# LOVER OF PREVIOUS
# BIRTH

# LOVER OF PREVIOUS
# BIRTH

Shyam Rathore

PARTRIDGE
A Penguin Random House Company

**To order additional copies of this book, contact**
Partridge India
000 800 10062 62
www.partridgepublishing.com/india

orders.india@partridgepublishing.com

# Contents

# Lover of Previous Birth

This novel is completely a work of fiction. There is no relation of it with any incident or event. Some incidence only belong to me. It begins with the story of a boy whose name is Vinay. In his previous birth, his name was Mohit. He loves Jaya Khan. In a previous birth, Jaya Khan lost Mohit (Vinay); the reason for it was that the Khan family was not happy about the love of Vinay and Jaya Khan. They killed Vinay and threw him in a well near a temple in the forest. However, Jaya did not leave Vinay and she jumped in a well after Vinay. Now in this birth, Jaya Khan is waiting for her lover at that well, where he had died in his previous birth. On this side, Vinay is the son of Dilip Shrivastav. Vinay is not the real son of Dilip Shrivastav. Dilip Shrivastav's wife found Vinay on a road. Vinay's mother likes Vinay very much and Vinay too likes his mother. Once Vinay becomes a part of the Shrivastav family, all their needs are fulfilled by God and they become rich. They gift a car to Vinay. In the middle of the story due to some reason Vinay's brother Raja tells Vinay that he is not the real son of Dilip Shrivastav. Then Vinay leaves home and goes to the city nearby. Tara and Vinay are friends from childhood and Tara loves Vinay too much.

She loves Vinay because they were friends in childhood and their marriage was fixed by their family, but Tara cannot get Vinay's love. Her wishes are not fulfilled. She feels that Rukhsar (sister of Jaya Khan) is taking Vinay away from her. A classmate of Vinay, Lalita, helps Vinay when unfortunately Vinay goes to jail; Lalita gives bail for Vinay. They become very good friends. Then Vinay does hard work to earn money by composing songs; after some days, Vinay gets married to Jaya Khan. However, Tara and Lalita only wait for Vinay's love. After some days, Vinay's album becomes a hit and he becomes a great singer.

Then Vinay shifts into his company's house. In this story, there is a little girl Payal also; she is the niece of Vinay. Rukhsar is the sister of Jaya Khan. After her parents' death, Rukhsar has to stay with her auntie; she has to listen to the taunts of her aunt due to Jaya Khan's marriage. And now this story starts from where Vinay lives with the Shrivastav family and studies in City College.

# Characters in Story

1. Vinay: Lover of Previous Birth
2. Jaya: Lover of Vinay
3. Lalita: Friend and Classmate of Vinay
4. Dilip Shrivastav: Father of Vinay
5. Shyam: Friend of Dilip
6. Ashif: Father of Rukhsar and Jaya
7. Samina: Mother of Rukhsar and Jaya
8. Amjad: Brother of Rukhsar and Jaya
9. Jai: Friend of Vinay
10. Tara: Fiancée of Vinay,
11. Payal: Five-Year-Old Daughter of Raja
12. Tanuj: Brother of Lalita
13. Archit: Classmate of Vinay
14. Anish and Aaysha: Children of Lalita and Archit
15. Badriprasad: Husband of Janki (Drunkard)
16. Khushilal: Friend of Badriprasad
17. Rukhsar: Sister of Jaya
18. K. L. Rathore: Boss of Vinay
19. Teena: Daughter of Roky Uncle
20. Salim: Husband of Rukhsar
21. Anjum Sheikh: Son of Aunt

# 1

# Vinay Goes to That Well and Temple about which He Used to Dream

Vinay: Father, I am going to city. I have to buy some books and clothes.

Father: You can go, but, my son, come in time. We will have dinner together in night.

Payal: Bring jalebi (favourite dish like sweet) for me.

Vinay: Where are my shoes?

Mother: Son, shoes are under the table. Go after having breakfast.

'Yes, Mom.'

Raja Bhaiya said, 'Vinay, you are going to city, so bring some goods for me. This is a list of goods which you have to bring.'

Mother said to Raja, 'Give money to Vinay.'

Raja gave some money to Vinay and said to him, 'Come in time.'

(Vinay was the younger son of Dilip Shrivastav. Vinay's parents loved Vinay very much. Vinay's mother loved Vinay so much that she could not eat food without

Vinay. Raja was the elder son of Dilip Shrivastav. He did not like the affection between Vinay and their mother. Payal is a six year daughter of Raja Bhaiya)

Vinay started his car and went to the city after having breakfast. After he left the village, he enjoyed the beauty of nature along the way. There was a dense forest in the way and the way was so narrow that only one four-wheeler could move at a time. The voice of birds could be heard very much in that area. If we saw a village from the hills, then it would look like a heaven. There were fields and land that look like green haven. There were cows, goats, sheep, and buffaloes grazing in the fields. After seeing such great scenery, Vinay was pleased to be there. There were dense hills and huge trees by the side of the road. There was a temple near a well; this well was quite old, and as nobody was near that well it looked scary. Its water had become black due to leaves of trees that had dropped in the well. This temple was under a banyan tree. But there was a beautiful tree near the temple, so it looked very good; because of huge trees, sunlight did not reach the tree and well properly. The weather was very cool. Because of this great scene, Vinay stopped his car for some time. Suddenly, a soft voice singing a song could be heard . . .

*Come, my beloved*
*Called my voice*
*I have waited for you being born again and again*
*I am sure you will come.*
*I will marry you*
*Come my . . . .*

*I have been searching for you for a long time.*
*I am living this life in your wait*
*Keep remembrance of mine for lifetime*
*Come my . . . .*
*After disunion I am very sad*
*You are my lover and beloved*
*I am waiting for you*
*Come my . . . .*
*You forget but I have remembered*
*This love story is not so easy*
*Keep me always in your eyes*
*Come, my beloved!*

Suddenly, Vinay recalled his past memories. He thought, 'This song has come many times in my dreams.' He thought, 'My destiny is calling me.' Then he went ahead.

There was a white temple. The same song could be heard again. Vinay saw a lion statue in the temple and he got nervous. His memory became fresh. Again he searched for the owner of the voice of the song. He went ahead. A large debris of leaves was around the temple. It seemed like nobody had come there for a long time. Then he went to the backside. There were steps to the temple. Then he went into the temple; he thought that he had come there many times. Then Vinay saw the well where he had died, but he didn't know about that secret. Vinay looked inside the well; it was dark inside. He picked up a piece of gravel (small piece of stone) and dropped it inside the well; the sound of dropping came after some time because it is very deep. Vinay felt some fear and thought something was there which connected with him. Then he saw that a beautiful girl was going away; her hair was black. He wanted to talk with her, but because of dense forest he neither went near her nor talked with her.

He came back and sat under the banyan tree. After some time, he fell asleep. Then again that song came in his dream and he became nervous. Suddenly, he came back to his car. Then he saw that a policeman was standing near his car.

He said, 'Oh, mister, where did you go for two hours? Nowadays, the time has changed. You should learn to keep your car safe. Otherwise you will lose this car this someday.'

'I am sorry, sir. I went to the temple to pray. Next time I will remember this.'

On listening to the respectful voice, the policeman became humble and thought, 'Nobody comes to pray here, then for what this boy came here?'

He started the car and went to the city. On the way, he again remembered that song. He thought about her.

'Who is she? Why is she important for me that I am thinking about her? Why is that well so scary?' Such kind of thoughts came in Vinay's mind.

'My heart is saying she is the one who is part of my life.'

After shopping for everything, he came back to the house. He thought, 'I should say to Mother about the incident that happened on the way. I have never spoken a lie to my mother in my life.' But he decided that this incident was not suitable to be spoken to his mother.

Just then, Payal came in running and asked, 'Open the bag fast and give me jalebi.'

Then Vinay said, 'First one papi (kiss), then I will give jalebi.' Then Vinay gave the things of Raja Bhaiya, which Vinay had brought from the city.

His mother said, 'Vinay, eat food.'

Vinay sat next to his mother and said, 'Mother, I will eat after some time.' Then after a few minutes he went to bed.

She was an affectionate and innocent mother; she knew that something was wrong with Vinay. She thought, 'He does not usually talk with me like that.' His mother entered his room and asked, 'What happened to you? Why are you sad? Are you OK?'

'Yes, Mom, I am OK.'

'Why are you hiding something from me? I am your mother, and you are my son. You have to share with me. Except me who else will solve your problem.'

Vinay: Mom, I am OK, Mom. No problem.

Then mother thought that he must be tired, and so he was looking like that.

Vinay thought about his mother and said, 'I realise that, Mother, you can read me in every situation. Mother, you are God. Don't keep me away from you in life. Otherwise I won't live. Mother, you love me very much. Why do you isolate Raja Bhaiya? Why don't you love Raja Bhaiya?'

Mother: He is also my son. But he doesn't obey me. As per his wife, he wants to take all property and he wants to live separate from us.

Vinay: Don't worry, Mom. I will instruct him.

His mother patted his head. He felt like he was in heaven because of his mother's love. It didn't cost anything,(love of mother is precious). His mind drifted to his childhood memories and he fell asleep.

Mother: Sleep after having dinner. You have gone to the city, but I know you didn't eat anything because you do not spend money on eating. We waited for you, but I knew that you would be late. See, I made your favourite dish.

'Oh, Mother, you are so good.' After having food, Vinay went to sleep.

He had a dream that four people were beating him. After some time, when he opened eyes he saw a statue of a lion. Then he wanted to go away from there. But the people came again and put him in the well. He cried loudly, 'Save me, save me.' But no one listened to the voice of Vinay.

Then suddenly he woke up and looked around, but no one was there. His face became wet with sweat.

After wiping his face, he slept again.

And again he got the dream of that girl. She was singing a song for Vinay.

*Come, my beloved*
*Called my heart*
*I have waited for you born and born*
*I am sure you will come.*

He became very upset and got up from his bed. Then his mother came. 'What happened, my son?'

And his mother patted his head again. 'Why are you so unhappy?'

Vinay: Mother, nothing. I am OK.

Mother: It cannot be possible. I can read you. You are not OK.

Vinay: I am not able to sleep due to a bad dream.

Then as Vinay slept next to his mother he fell asleep.

His mother patted his head. All his problems and worry were gone. Then he said in dominion (in sleeping state), 'Mother is earth, Mother is sky, Mother is river, Mother is lake. My mother's love is bigger than all the world.'

Then his mother said, 'What are you saying? I am proud that my son gives me so respect.'

In the morning, Vinay woke up and touched his parents' feet; after that, he got ready for bath. After bathing, he sat on a chair and thought about the day before's incident. Again in his mind came that song.

Then he thought, 'What is the secret in this song after all?' Due to such a thought, he got nervous. He wanted to forget this problem. So he passed more time with Payal and his mother.

But whenever he thought about that girl and her song, he again got nervous.

Gradually, he forgot that incident as he got busy with his family. And he wanted to forget too this incident.

Vinay wanted to become a singer from childhood. He started writing a dairy when he was eight years old. Vinay's aim was that he would like to become a singer.

# 2

# Vinay Meets Rukhsar and Lalita in College

The next day when he went to college his eyes were caught by the words on the notice board. He saw that the annual function would take place in the college the next day. He was happy that he could give his name for singing. His friends asked Vinay, 'You will sing a song?'

Vinay said, 'Why can I not?'

Then his friend Archit said, 'Why should you not? You can sing. We are saying because you are for the first time singing in college. You have not told us before today that you like singing.'

'Yes, Archit, you are right.'

Jay said, 'Today I found for the first time that Vinay is not only a good student but also singer.'

After class, Vinay went back home. He explained to his mother that he had written his name for singing for the annual function. And he was going to sing for the first time.

'Vinay, you will sing a song?'

'Yes, Mother, I am.'

'Which song you will sing?'

*'Come, my beloved*

*Calling my heart . . . .'*

'I think, Vinay, this song is very old. I haven't heard this song.'

'No, Mother, this is a new song.'

After the conversation with his mother, he started practising for his song. In two hours, his song was ready.

The next day, the function started at ten o'clock. Then Vinay started singing his song. All the students knew that Vinay was such a good singer too, and everyone knew that Vinay's voice was very melodious. For the first time, they were listening to his painful (sad) song. But Vinay forgot the last line of the song. So all became quiet at that time. After ten seconds, a blue-eyed pretty girl completed the last line of the song. Everyone clapped after listening to this lovely song. He was quite a lot of respect. And then he came down from stage and searched for that girl. After listening to her sweet voice, he thought, 'Who is she?' Vinay ran fast before she disappeared like before. He searched for her; she could not be seen. Then he turned back; after that, he saw that pretty girl. Her hair was black and curly. Vinay sensed that his dream girl had come in his life. His search and wait was over now.

Vinay thanked that pretty girl and said, 'Today you have saved me. I had forgotten the last line of song and you helped me in singing a song.'

His niece, Payal, said to Vinay, 'You are saved on stage by this angel.'

Vinay said to that pretty girl, 'I have seen you in college first time. Are you a new admission?'

'Yes, you are right. I am a new admission. My name is Rukhsar.'

Vinay thought, 'She is that girl who met me at the old temple, but that day I couldn't see her face.'

Meanwhile Payal said to Vinay, 'Uncle, who is she? She is an angel.'

'No, Payal, she is a girl. She is like an angel.'

'Uncle, she is very beautiful.'

'Payal, you are beautiful too.'

Then Payal and Vinay were ready to go back home. But his eyes kept searching for Rukhsar. It seemed to him as if his dream girl was going away from him. He was thinking, 'I should have taken her number and address. How will I see her now?'

Then Vinay and Payal reached home. Vinay said to his mother, 'Today I sang a song, Mother.'

At once Payal said, 'Grandma, Uncle had forgotten the last line of song.'

'Then what happened?' his mother said.

'Then a pretty girl completed that line. She saved Uncle on stage otherwise Uncle . . . .'

'I think you haven't completely by heart,' his mother said.

'Yes, you are right, Mom. I haven't practised properly, so I forgot.'

He thought, 'This mistake is very important for me. Who is she? Rukhsar and the girl at the temple are same. Because except her nobody know that song which I have heard at old temple. At stage in collage she has completed last line of song also. I should have met with her.'

The next day he went to college and asked the reception madam about Rukhsar. He said to the madam, 'Yesterday at the function a girl completed my song. Her name is Rukhsar. Do you have address or mobile number of her?'

Madam said, 'Rukhsar couldn't pay her fee, so she couldn't get admission in college. Even I don't have any receipt document of her address or mobile number. Go to the accounts head. Maybe you will get some information from there about her.' After listening about Rukhsar that she couldn't pay the fees for her admission in college he became sad and thought that he should help her.

Then Vinay went to the accounts department and asked Babu sir, 'I need the address of Rukhsar.'

First Babu sir refused to give Vinay her address, and he said, 'We don't have permission to give address to anyone.'

In Vinay's college, not only Babu sir but also everyone knew that Vinay was a very good-natured person.

Babu sir realised then that no one refused him because Vinay was a very good student and he was asking for only a valid reason. Hence, Babu sir was ready to give the address of Rukhsar to Vinay.

Vinay became very happy after he got the address of Rukhsar. Then he started the car and went to Rukhsar's village. He asked some people where was Rukhsar's house. They said, 'We don't know.' So Vinay couldn't find Rukhsar. Then finally he went to an old man and asked him respectfully.

The old man said that they had left that house the day before. 'But tell me, gentleman, who is she to you?'

Vinay replied to the old man, 'She is my all. I mean she is dream girl. I cannot live without her. Please give me address of her. Where has she gone?'

The old man said, 'I don't have the number or address of them.'

After Vinay had gone away, the people talked among themselves. 'That gentleman has gone crazy.'

Another man said, 'I think he is a *lover of previous birth.*'

Vinay became sad as Rukhsar could not be found. And he came back home. His mother realised, 'My son has some problem. He always looks worried.' Then his mother asked him, 'What is your problem? What are you worrying about?'

Vinay said to his mother, 'I will tell you an appropriate time.'

But Vinay's mother thought, 'What is the problem? Why is he not telling me?' She thought it was his personal problem.

Then when Vinay fell asleep at night he had a dream of that girl. Vinay saw that girl at the well which was near the temple.

Vinay said to that girl, 'You are very beautiful, do you know? Payal is right. You are just like an angel. But in your eyes I can see my love.'

Then she cast down her eyes and gave a little smile.

Then Vinay sang a song for her.

*Secret meeting was incomplete*
*Come, spring, with new morning*
*You make me mad by love*
*Infest me day and night*
*You are my morning of destinies*
*Meeting . . . !*
*Your eyes are mirror of love*
*Your body like marble*
*Hair are black and bright your cheek*
*I am crazy for your young age*
*Heart is watch. Think about you*
*Meeting . . . !*
*Our love is for birth and birth*
*I lost my heart in your love*
*Your hair is like cloud*
*Eyes are calling me always*
*Without you everywhere fog*
*Meeting . . . !*

Suddenly he got up and looked around, but he couldn't even see her shadow. Now Vinay fell in love with that girl. Vinay's eyes looks tearful by love and separation of that girl. He always felt that Rukhsar would come. His dream girl would come now. Vinay looked at the door and thought that she was coming. His eyes searched for a picture of that girl in the air. Now it seemed that Rukhsar was the girl who had come in dream. His eyes were searching for her like he had lost something.

His mother too thought that someone had done magic on her son.

His mother said to Vinay, 'Don't worry, my son, and pay attention on your studies.'

'OK, Mom, please keep me always with you.'

The next day Vinay went to the studio and said to the director, 'I want to make an album of my songs.' And he showed him his writing work.

Then he replied to Vinay, 'You have to pay ten thousand rupees for music expense. If you will arrange, then I am ready otherwise you can go now.'

Vinay knew basic computers so he started a job at Roky Uncle's cyber cafe. Before Vinay, this job was handled by Teena. She is the daughter of Roky Uncle. She had given training to Vinay and Vinay learnt all of the work in two days.

Vinay had handled a job in college time. However, Vinay had not told to his mother about the job. Vinay wanted ten thousand rupees for his composed song as soon as possible.

One day, Vinay made a plan to go to the city for a good job.

Vinay asked his mother, 'Mother, I am going to city.'

His mother thought, 'He is sad since many days and hasn't informed me what the problem is. Whenever he goes outside, he becomes so unhappy.' She said to Vinay, 'Where are you going? You want to live separate from us?'

'No, Mother, I am going for some work. I will come back soon. Can I take your mobile too?'

Vinay's mother said, 'Yes, you can take my mobile.'

Payal said to Vinay, 'Uncle, I want to come with you too.'

'OK, Payal, come and sit in the car.'

Then they departed from home. On the way, they came to the forest. Vinay stopped the car at the well which was near the temple. And they went towards the temple. Once Vinay went ahead towards the temple, Payal said to Vinay 'Where are we going, Uncle?'

Then the voice of that girl could be heard . . .

*Come, my beloved, calling my heart . . . .*

They heard that song. After listening to the song, Payal asked Vinay, 'You have sung this song at the college.'

'Yes, you are right. Come with me to search for that girl.'

Vinay sang a song for her.

*Oh, my lover, please stop.*
*Listen my heart speaks*
*We are both one*
*Keep it in your heart*

But she did not stop and she was gone.

'Come, Payal, we will definitely search for her.' They followed the sound of the girl. But suddenly a call came on Vinay's phone.

His mother said, 'Come immediately, my son. Guests have come for your engagement.'

Vinay felt that it was a new problem for him.

After some time, they reached home. Vinay greeted the guests respectfully.

They asked Vinay, 'How are you doing in studies?'

'I am doing well.'

Suddenly Payal came in between and said, 'Grandpa, today we saw the temple . . .'

Vinay was afraid that she would tell the guests about that girl. So immediately he said, 'Come here, take this chocolate.' He whispered in her ears, 'Don't say to this anyone otherwise I will neither take you to the city nor bring jalebi.'

'OK, Uncle, I won't say to this anyone.'

Vinay's mother said to the guests, 'How do you like my son?'

'He is very innocent like a cow.'

'Yes, you are right. Vinay is one among million. He is the best, they said, 'We like Vinay.'

Vinay was afraid that they knew about his misdeed of that day. But the guests already knew about Vinay because Vinay's class teacher was a friend of the guests. He had told them about Vinay.

Vinay's mother said, 'So are you agreeing for this relationship?'

The guests said, 'Yes, we are OK.'

Vinay's mother said, 'Meet Tara tomorrow. In childhood, you have already met Tara. But one more time you should meet Tara because we don't want any problem in future in this relationship. Till now everything is in your hand.' Then in the evening the guests had gone.

Vinay said to his mother, 'Mother, you want me to be separated from you? After marriage, you will be separated from me. I cannot live without you, so I will not marry in life.'

'No, my son, this is a law of society, which all have to accept.'

'Mother, you are saying, so I am ready otherwise I will not marry.'

Vinay always respected his mother's order.

On the other hand, Vinay's hard work had made him successful. The next day, Vinay would be getting his salary. Due to this, Vinay was very happy.

The next day he thought, 'I have to collect salary, but also I have to attend class.' So he went to college and attended the class. He was passing by a classroom when his eyes were caught by some boys. They were standing. A beautiful girl too was standing there. She was asking the guys about the principal's office. But they told the wrong way to that girl. Vinay knew that the guys were not good. They always troubled new admissions. Immediately, Vinay came and said, 'You are asking for principal's office, so go straight and move left, then you will find principal's office. They told you the direction to the toilet.'

'They are not good guys,' she said angrily.

'Yes, you are right. Their mothers have not taught them good manners,' Vinay said.

'But you look like a good person. You stay there. I will just come after meeting with the principal. Wait here. I need your help.

After some time, she came.

Vinay asked her, 'Your meeting with the principal was a success?'

'Yes, my work is done. What is your name?' she said, smiling.

'My name is Vinay. And what is your name?'

'My name is Lalita. Let's go.'

Then they boys said, 'Madam, did you find the principal's room?'

'I got it,' she said angrily.

'These guys are not good,' Vinay said to Lalita.

'Yes, you are right.'

Then one boy said, 'Oh, what's going on? Champu (most intelligent) with girl?'

Then Vinay said, 'You did not show the right way to the girl and you trouble new admissions.'

'Oh, you understand yourself to be a hero? You sang a song in that programme and you consider yourself to be a hero.'

Then Vinay said to those boys, 'I will give you a warning. My song will come out in the market one day definitely. Then Lalita said, 'Let's go, Vinay. Don't make enemies because of me.'

After that, they both reached the park, and Lalita asked Vinay about classes, times, and subjects. Vinay explained everything about college to Lalita.

'My brother is coming from Delhi today. I am going to receive him. Please come with me. I haven't seen the station. Please come with me,' said Lalita.

Then Vinay said, 'I cannot come with you because I have to collect salary. Today is my salary day. So I have to go there.'

'OK, no problem. I will come with you, then both works will be done.'

# 3

# Vinay Goes to Jail and
# Lalita Gives Bail

Lalita started car and they both went first to collect Vinay's salary.

Lalita said to Vinay, 'We have to get back in time otherwise Bhaiya would feel bad.'

'OK, stop car here,' Vinay said to Lalita.

He came out the car and went to Roky Uncle for his salary.

Roky Uncle said to Vinay, 'Come inside.'

Then Roky Uncle got Vinay beaten by a rascal.

He put the blame on Vinay that he had teased his daughter Teena.

After listening to this, Lalita came too. She could not tolerant this. She said angrily to Teena, 'Vinay cannot do such a misdeed. But you have definitely done this.'

Then Vinay said to Roky Uncle, 'If you don't want to give money, no problem, but why do you blame me about Teena? You don't know my father is Dilip Shrivastav? If he will come to know about me, then what will he think about me? Asking for money from home is not good for me, so I have taken a job here. But you have made my value zero.' They couldn't reply to Vinay. After some time, the police come and Vinay was arrested.

On the other hand, Lalita went to the station to meet her brother, Tanuj.

Vinay could not sleep in jail. His mother was quite disturbed because of Vinay. She was thinking about Vinay where he had gone and why he didn't come home still.

Over there, Vinay was thinking too, 'I have done job at Roky Uncle and I didn't inform my parents about this job and today I am in jail. If my mother comes to know this, she will feel very bad. And what will they think about me?'

Then Vinay's mother made a call to Vinay's college and asked about Vinay. She told them that he had not come home. Then they told Vinay's mother that they had seen him yesterday and that he had gone with Lalita, and they also gave the contact number of Lalita to Vinay's mother. Then Vinay's mother made a call to Lalita, and she explained to Vinay's mother, 'He is with me and he is all right. Don't worry. Right now he is in the bathroom.' Then she disconnected the call. His mother was quite disturbed because of Vinay; she thought that Vinay had not told her what the problem was after all.

On the other hand, Lalita arranged some money for bail of Vinay. Then Vinay came out of jail. As Lalita knew that Vinay was hungry as he had not eaten since the night before, so they went to a good restaurant for food.

Then Vinay said to Lalita, 'People are not good. You have helped me. I will never forget it. From today you are my best friend.'

After listening to this sentence, Lalita become very happy. She said, 'Vinay, this is my duty. And we all have to help each other. Otherwise there is no use of this life.

'You are right, Lalita, but some people in this world are not good. Yesterday, the boys disturbed you in college and today Roky Uncle and Teena blamed me and also sent me to jail. Now I will take care of myself from such people. Why God does send me among such people? Lalita, I went to jail for the first time. Mosquitoes bit me yesterday night.'

'This is rule of life. On the way of truth, many troubles come in life. You don't worry, Vinay. Good friends always help each other.'

'But my family should not know about this incident otherwise it will not be good for me. I will be zero in front of my family. And if Rukhsar comes to know, it will be great trouble for me and she will never see my face,' said Vinay.

'Who is Rukhsar?' asked Lalita.

'Oh, Lalita, I didn't tell you. She is my lover. My heart beats whenever I remember her. My heart always thinks about her. I don't know when she will meet me. I can't live without her. Lalita, I feel that she is not only my breath but also lover of my previous birth.'

'You love her so much? OK, enough.' And she stopped the conversation about Rukhsar. She said,

31

'Yesterday your mother called me. She was asking about you. "Where is Vinay?" I said to her, "He is all right and with me. He will come home very soon. Don't worry about him."

They are talking when in between their conversation a call came again. Vinay's mother asked, 'Where is Vinay and when will he come back?'

Lalita said, 'He is here. Please talk with him.'

'Hello, my son, how are you? I am quite disturbed because of you. Have you eaten food?'

'Yes, Mother, I am good. I was in a marriage of one of my friends. I am really sorry I didn't inform you. Are you all right, Mother?'

'Yes, I am good, but you take care of yourself. Tell me, who is Lalita? You don't inform me nowadays.'

'I will tell you at home.'

'OK, my son, come soon. I am waiting for you.'

'OK, I am just coming. Let's go, Lalita, to my home. My mother is waiting.'

Then they reached home.

Then his mother said, 'People say right that girls separate son from his mother. Vinay, after your marriage, don't go away from me.'

'OK, Mother. How are you?' Vinay said.

His mother said, 'My son, see today I have cooked your favourite dish. And I know that you were hungry. So I was waiting for you. And you seem tired today. What is the matter after all?'

'Yes, Mom, you are saying right. I am tired. I went to attend a marriage of one of my friends, and so you are quite disturbed because of me. Please forgive me, my mother.'

As they were talking, Lalita said, 'I am quite happy to see the lovely relationship between mother and son.' She thought, 'If my mother were in my life, she would have loved me too like that. But such love is not in my life.'

Lalita said, 'OK, Vinay, I am going.'

'No, go after having food.'

'No, I will be late.'

'Then have tea.' Vinay's sister-in-law made tea; in the meanwhile, they started talking again. 'My son, before today you haven't gone without informing me. How did you go without asking me this time? You didn't even call me the next day.'

'Mother, I already told you I am very sorry. I had forgotten to inform you. I will remember this incident and never do it the next time.'

Mother said, 'My son, I am just asking only.'

Then Lalita said, 'My brother is waiting for me. I have to go now.'

Then they had their tea and Lalita went to her house.

Then Vinay said to his mother, 'Mom, Lalita is a very good girl.'

'You are talking like that as she saved you from great trouble.'

'No, Mother, it is not such a matter.'

'Yes, it is right. Love of a mother is less than a girl's love.'

Vinay said, 'You are greater than God.'

'Don't think such things about me.'

'People are not good, Mom.'

'What is the matter?' his mother said.

'Mom, yesterday in college some boys were troubling Lalita.'

'You are again starting her topic.'

'OK, I am sorry. Now I will not talk about her.'

Then his mother said, 'Yesterday Roky and Teena had come. They were quite sad and saying, "Please forgive us." They didn't say more what was the matter. I don't know. Vinay, are you hiding something from me?'

'I am sorry, Mother. I didn't tell you I have done a job at Roky Uncle's cyber cafe. I have sung a song in the college, so I had to compose that song. I didn't want to ask for money from you.'

Vinay's mother said, 'You seem to think that I am separate from you, and so you have not taken money from the house. My son, this is your home and wealth, and why are you thinking like that? Next time don't do like that.'

'OK, Mother, I will never do this again,' said Vinay.

'Roky cheated you so God has given punishment to him. His shop was destroyed in fire. They have given ten thousand rupees too,' his mother said.

Vinay said, 'For this money, Roky Uncle cheated with me.'

# 4

# Raja Quarrels with Vinay
# and Vinay Leaves Home

Vinay's mother and Vinay were talking when Raja Bhaiya came and said, 'Mother, I need five thousand rupees. I have to bring goods for our shop.'

But Raja's wife had told to Vinay's mother that Payal's father (Raja) used to have wine and gambled too. After listen to his words, his mother became unhappy. She knew that her son was not in control now.

Then Vinay said, 'Raja Bhaiya, please don't ask for money from Mother. You are elder, so you should have to think.'

'You keep quiet!'

'Don't be angry, Bhaiya. Take five thousand rupees.'

Then their mother said to Vinay, 'Don't give the money to Raja. You have earned this money with effort. And this money too you earned for your song's album, not for wine and gambling. Vinay, you don't know yesterday he lost ten thousand rupees by gambling. And he also wasted money on wine.'

'Brother, this is too much.

Mother, you shouldn't give money to Bhaiya. Take care in future.'

Raja said to Vinay, 'What are you saying now? Think before speaking. You don't know anything about yourself. I think the time has come that you should know your own value. Till today you don't know who you are. You are not the son of Dilip Shrivastav. You don't know that my mother had brought you from the road. And you incite my parents against me?'

After listening to this, it seemed to Vinay as if someone had slapped to him.

Vinay's mother got angry and she slapped Raja and said, 'You have gone crazy. What have you said?'

Vinay's sister-in-law said, 'Oh God, what happened to him today? This is unbelievable. How can he use such cheap language with Vinay?'

Vinay immediately came and touched his mother's feet and said, 'There is no mother in the world like you. You love me more than Bhaiya even though I am not your real son.'

His mother said, 'Vinay, you are my real son. Whatever Raja said is not true. Don't believe him. You know he's drunk and has lost his senses. So he has said nonsense words. Don't worry. I am your real mother.'

A flood of tears flowed down Vinay's eyes. For a moment, he felt that there was no one in the world with him.

Then he remembered Rukhsar and Lalita. It seemed to him that only Lalita and Rukhsar were his friends.'

But she is my mother. How can I go away from her? How can I live without her? My life is my fate and everyone makes fun of me.' And he laughed at himself.

Then his mother said, 'Don't go away from me. Except you, no one listens to me. Only you understand me. I am proud of you, my son.'

'Mother, you care so much for me. Please don't say anything to Raja Bhaiya after leaving me. He is right. I would have known it sometime in future. You have changed my life. You have taught me such good manners so that I will never face any problem or trouble. This is a great obiligaiton for me. But how I will pay up this debt that has been take care of me since childhood

Mom, take care of yourself. My destiny is calling me.' Saying this, he touched his mother's feet. 'I should go now.'

Vinay's heart was weeping for his mother. He was going away from his mother, who had loved him every moment.

Then Payal came and said to Vinay, 'Don't go, Uncle. I cannot live without you. you will not stay here with us, then who will take me the city and who will bring jalebi for me?'

Vinay said to Payal, 'Papa will give jalebi. You don't worry. Pay attention to your studies. I will not be there, so you study in Grandma's room from today. Don't go in the sunlight. You have to wait for some time. I will come very soon.'

Payal said, 'Don't go, Uncle. Don't go, Uncle.' her face become sad.

Then Payal's mother came and told Vinay, 'Payal's father is drunk, so please forgive him and ignore it. Don't go. Don't take seriously his words. What will we tell our relative who is coming tomorrow for your engagement? You also have to go there to see your fiancée, who is waiting for you.'

Vinay said, 'Please forgive me if I have done mistakes with all of you.'

Finally, he touched his father's feet and started to go. Then his father said, 'I know this that where you will go you will get your destiny, but without you this house will be lonely.'

Then his mother came and gave him ten thousand rupees and said to Vinay, 'Finally you have showed that you've become a stranger. I have never consider you stranger But now you have become my step son.

'Mother, what are you saying? And you understand me to be a stranger so you are saying such words. But you don't understand me as a stranger. My destiny is calling me. I am going to do something. I will be a good man with blessings of you all.'

Finally, Vinay left home. Then he made a call to Lalita and said bye to her. She was shocked. 'Why are you doing this, you know?' she asked him. 'Where are you going after all?'

Then Vinay said to her, 'I am going to my destiny who is calling me. Take care of yourself. Boys are not good in college.'

She said, 'I will take care of myself, but you also take care of yourself.' Then he left for the city in search of a job to earn money and help him compose his song to make an album.

But Lalita thought, 'What happened to Vinay. Where is he going? His mother loves him very much, then why has he left home.'

After Vinay left home, Payal became upset. She said to her father, 'I will never talk with you. My uncle have gone from here because of you only' Raja felt much regret on hearing this. On the other hand, Vinay's mother's health too became poor. His mother would not eat food on time without Vinay now. She always thought that where her son had gone and he must be hungry and thirsty.

When Raja awakened, he felt regret. He destroyed his honour in his own view. 'Due to wine I have separated my brother from me, a son from his mother, and a niece from his uncle. This wine not only destroys me but also this world. I will never touch wine in my life.'

Raja went to his mother and held her feet and said, 'I will never do such a mistake in life. You don't worry. He has gone due to me and I will bring him too. I will never do any other mistake in my life. It is my promise.'

His mother didn't reply. He felt guilty of himself. He knew that because of him his mother and daughter were disturbed. However, he felt that he had done a great mistake. He made a commitment to himself that he would change himself. So in a few days, he changed himself. His father had a lot of money, but he started doing a job. He took care of his mother like Vinay. He left wine and gambling. After Vinay left home, Raja did all work like Vinay, but he could not remove sadness of Payal and his mother.

On the other hand, Vinay was sad all the time. Vinay could not live away from his mother just like his mother could not live away from her son Vinay. He thought 'Maybe I have committed sins in life so I deserve to stay away from my mother's love. This is a circumstance which would change my life and complete my destiny also.' Then he reminded himself, 'I have no mother. She has brought me up and taught me such good manners. She loves me so much. This debt neither I nor God can repay, because her love is precious. Mother is divine because of her affection. Her behaviour is like Sharda Maa (Goddess of Knowledge). All of Vinay's work would be complete after remembering his mother's name. She always prayed for her son.

# 5

# Breaks Off Engagement with Tara

Vinay's father had sent news to Tara's father, Shyam, that they were breaking off the engagement of Tara and Vinay. After listening to this news, Tara's father lost his senses. He said to Vinay's father, 'What is the reason that you are breaking off this engagement? It cannot be possible. Please tell me the reason.' Vinay's father didn't reply to him. Tara's father understood that it could be some big reason, and so Vinay's father said that they were breaking up Vinay and Tara's engagement.

After listening to this news, the fiancée of Vinay, Tara, became crazy. She had loved Vinay since childhood. She was sure that her fiancé was the only one meant for her, so she became angry and came to Vinay's home and asked Vinay's mother, 'You have broken off our love in a second. My love is only for Vinay. I have waited too much. He is not only my lover but also my beloved. I beg you to give me back my life. This life is useless without Vinay. You know that our alliance was fixed in childhood and till now I haven't thought about anyone other than Vinay. I love him very much. All this happened in front of you. And even you know this that we like each other. Only one thing is that Vinay didn't tell me that he loves me. It does not mean that he doesn't love me. Otherwise this relationship is not strong till date. You must give me back my love.'

Then Vinay's mother said, 'You don't know that when he was a baby I had brought him up. Now listen to your Vinay's story. One day, Vinay's father and I were coming from the city. Suddenly, we heard the voice of a child. Then we saw a child was weeping. I couldn't bear to see him weeping. I went to him and took him in my arms. We thought that his mother had gone somewhere, and she would come to take this child in some time. We waited a long time, but nobody came to take the child. Then we brought Vinay home. We brought up Vinay. He is my heart. He is always in my thoughts. His antics are in my eyes. And you are saying, "Give me back my love"? You don't know how much I love him. You have loved him only, but I have fed him milk. God help my son. I am the only one in this world who belongs to Vinay, but I know he cannot live without me. My affection will bring him. He will come very soon here.'

Then Tara said, 'I have considered Vinay as my husband, he also belongs to me. Now what may I see but I'll never change my decision about Vinay.'

Then Payal came and said, 'Vinay uncle loves a girl. Her name is Rukhsar. Uncle likes Rukhsar very much. The day your father came here for engagement of Uncle, that day I and Vinay Uncle went to an old temple to search for Rukhsar. Then Grandma called us to say that Vinay Uncle had to come home immediately as some guest had come to see him. Then I and Uncle came back home.'

After listening to this story, Tara knew that this was the reason for the break off their engagement. But she didn't know actually what was the reason for the break off of her engagement and also didn't know about Vinay that he had left home due to Raja Bhaiya and Vinay's quarrel. She understood that Vinay had gone for studies in the city. Then she said to Vinay's mother, 'Rukhsar does not belong to our religion. Even then you are ready to accept this relation of Vinay and Rukhsar?'

Then Vinay's mother said, 'My son has gone away from me and you are troubling me. This is not fair.'

Tara's eyes became wet after listening to Vinay's mother's words. She understood that Rukhsar was standing in her way. Vinay loved Rukhsar; it is clear from Payal's words. But Tara did not take this seriously. She thought, 'I will definitely win my Vinay's heart. We haven't met since long, so he has forgotten me. Whenever he will meet me, our love will become like the time before.'

Vinay's mother read Tara's sad face and said to her, 'See, Tara, it depends on my son. I cannot see my son sad.'

Then Payal said, 'Grandma, Uncle had told me not to share this with someone. But after listening to your conversation I have to say.'

Vinay started to search for a job in the nearest town, because he needed ten thousand rupees to give to the director for composing his song. Due to this requirement, he thought that he had to do a job at any cost. Then after a long search, he got labour work. Vinay had to look after his own expenses apart from the ten thousand rupees. So he made a plan to search for some smart work. But that day, he got a hundred rupees after working in intense sunlight. Then he realised how he have earned this hundred rupees, he knew the value of a hundred rupee after doing hard work. He thought, 'I know this today. This is obligation of my parents that I have learnt computers. Otherwise, I would have to do such kind of job too.'

Vinay had done his computer course. So he started searching a job in the computer field. After a few days, he got a job in the computer field. Now he started to go for work and along with that he saved time for study too. He clearly knew how we should use time in the right way. Otherwise, we would have to repent.

He had already taken a good room. He cooked food himself. How one could save their time could be learnt from Vinay. First, he cut vegetables, then put vegetables in hot refined oil. While the vegetables cooked, he would knead the flour and roll to make bread. Then he baked the bread one by one and ate also. Then he went to office; however, he saved time for his destiny. He knew that time never came after passing. His first task was to arrange ten thousand rupees so that he could give to the director for making the song. So he thought, 'After studying, I will compose a song.'

One day, he made a call to Lalita. She was happy to get a call from Vinay. She thought, 'There is something between us, so he is calling me.'

Then he said, 'How are you?'

'I am fine. What about you?' said Lalita.

'I am good. Can you tell me about exam date?'

And Lalita said to Vinay, 'Write down the exam date.'

Then Vinay said, 'Write down my address. Please send me my admit card to this address.'

Vinay thanked Lalita.

Lalita said to Vinay, 'There is no need to say thanks, please. I made you my friend, so I know how to adjust to this friendship.'

However, Lalita wanted to talk to Vinay for a long time, but Vinay felt that she was passing time only. And also he hadn't the money, so he disconnected the call. And Vinay came back to his room.

After Vinay left the telephone booth, Lalita made a call there for Vinay. But she got the reply that it was a telephone booth and many people call from there.

Lalita became sad to hear this. She thought, 'How shall I talk to Vinay now?' Then she remembered, 'I have address of him, so I can go there to meet him.'

Now that Vinay knew his exam time table, so he started to study for exam. He studied till night and got up early morning for study also. He knew that morning time good for study, and there is much chance of success in morning time study, because in mornings our minds are fresh, so our minds absorb knowledge easily.

After some days, he got his admit card. Lalita had told all students in the college that Vinay was coming for exams. She told Vinay's parents too. Vinay's family became happy to hear this good news.

On the date of the exam, he comes home to his parents and touches the feet of his father and mother. Vinay's mother said to Vinay, 'Come back after the exam.'

Vinay went to college. In the college, he saw that some mannerless boys were standing there, the same who had teased Lalita when she came to college the first time. And from the other side, a handicapped boy was coming. They laughed at the boy; they commented on his low caste too. Then Vinay said to the boys, 'You have still not changed. You don't know that our body is given by God and our caste is also given by God, so we should not insult anyone. God drives our life and he can stop any time, so respect everyone as they all created by God. We should not laugh at such people, but we have to enhance confidence of such people. We should respect women and old men. Last time you made a joke at Lalita. You should have known that when people worship women God stays there. This is written in books of six class. But you haven't followed it. Not only men, we should also take care of animals and love them and never hurt them because they are all sons of God.'

After listening to Vinay's speech, the boys came to Vinay and said, 'Please forgive us. There is a need in this college for people like you.'

Then Vinay met all his friends and said to them, 'You all study with heart. Because this life is very small and our task is very big. So do effort in life. Always keep in mind your destiny.'if we don't consider an aim in life, it means we are living this life like useless.

After exams, he went to his home. Vinay was happy to meet his parents. Payal came and sat in Vinay's lap and said, 'Don't go now. Please stay here with us. After you left home, no one plays with me. Only you played with me.' She said to her grandma, 'Please convey to Uncle to stay here with us.'

After listening to Payal, Vinay's mother's eyes became wet. She wiped her eyes and said, 'My son, how your health had changed. Do you not eat food at time?'

Vinay said, 'Mother, I don't like city food.'

Then she said to him, 'Come, my son, have food. You must be hungry.'

Then everyone in the family had food together. Vinay's mother said to Vinay, 'Don't go now. See, it is a very good sight. All our family is here. Without you, this family is not complete. If you will not stay here, then I will consider that you don't assume me to be your real mother even now.'

Vinay's eyes got wet to see this great affection of his mother. Payal saw Vinay's face and said, 'Don't go, Uncle.'

Then Payal's mom (Vinay's sister-in-law) came and said to Vinay, 'Payal does not eat food in time and doesn't study on time too. She is always talking about you. She keeps saying, "When my uncle will come? When my uncle will come?" And your brother (Raja) is totally changed. Now he has become like you. He has started following your good manners now. He has left wine and gambling.'

Vinay seemed pleased that his brother had changed. After talking with his mother and sister-in-law, Vinay came to his father. He said to him, 'Staying away from you is very difficult. Every step I remember you. I found out how to affort in life after staying away, And I find out that which have taught me is very important for me.' Vinay's father was happy to listen to Vinay's sentence; he felt that someone was there too who followed him. They talked for some time.

And Vinay thought, 'I have to go back.' But he saw that his mother was looking very happy because he was there. He said to his mother, 'Be happy always like this.'

His mother said to Vinay, 'How did you stay alone there? You didn't think about us here.'

Then Vinay said, 'Yes, every time I think about you. But what can I do? I would like to become a singer, so I am doing effort there. I want to make you proud.'

After talking some time, he said to his mother, 'If you permit me, can I use the car?'

Then Vinay's mother said, 'This car is only for you. Nobody drives it after you left house. It is waiting for you too and saying that when will my Vinay come back.' Then they laughed.

Vinay said, 'Mother, you always keep smiling like this.' After talking to his mother, he went out and got inside the car.

# 6

# Vinay Meets Jaya Khan
# for the First Time

Vinay drove the car to the well in the forest, where he had seen his beloved for the first time. He stopped the car, and then he went ahead toward the temple. He waited for a long time for her there. But he saw nobody there; after some time, Vinay heard that same voice.

*I have been waiting for a long time.*
*Come, my beloved, calling my heart . . . .*

Vinay was happy when he heard the song; he wanted to try and go near that girl. He felt that if she went away without talking him it would not be good for him. Finally he reached that girl and he asked, 'Who are you?'

She replied, 'I am Shivangini.'

Vinay said, 'I have seen you many times in my dream. Why do you come here? I dreamt this song which you sing. In my dream, I feel that someone is calling me.'

She realised, 'He is the one for me. I have been waiting for him many years. Now he has come.'

Then she replied to Vinay, 'I came here to search for my lover Mohit. Some people didn't like our love in our previous birth so they killed Mohit in my previous birth and they threw him in that well. Then I jumped too here. It was the end of our love story. Now you have come and I got my love. My wish is fulfilled. I knew it that you will come here.'

'But why had they ended our love?' Vinay asked.

'I will tell you this at an appropriate time,' she said.

'What is your name in this birth?'

'My name is Jaya Khan. In my previous birth, my name was Shivangini,' she replied.

'But how do you remember this from the previous birth?' Vinay asked.

Jaya said, 'This is a result of my meditation and austerity. I have done this only for you.'

Vinay said, 'How does it happen?'

Jaya said, 'For this state we have to sit in thoughtless and awareness state to connect with the power of Almighty. This is the special power of God which resides in everyone, but we have to raise it. By this, we can do anything. And this is used only for welfare.'but only some people reach this state who believe in almighty power.

Vinay realised that Jaya was right. He had got to know that there was no one else but she whom he was searching for. And he had dreamt of her. He got to know the secret of the well; it was the place he had died. He got the answer of that question why he dreamt of the old well. He was satisfied.

Vinay said, 'I salute your love. You have done this only for me. Really, you have done a great job and you have been waiting for me so.'

Jaya said, 'You are right. We have met after a long time. I am waiting for this special time for many years now. Don't leave me and don't go away from me. Let's go to my home.'

Vinay said, 'Not now, but I will definitely come to your home. It is my pleasure that I got you, but I have to give our love the right direction. I mean I have to make my career too so that our future will be bright I don't have anything to give you happiness right now. So we have to wait for some time for our wedding.'

Jaya said, 'I will wait for you.'

Vinay said, 'I have to go near the town. Will you come with me?'

'No, I cannot come with you because I have to take care of my father all the time. He is not well,' she said.

Vinay said, 'I dreamt of you, and now I realise that you are my destiny. Is it our love?'

'Yes, this is the identification of our love,' she said.

'Where do you live?' Vinay asked.

'I live in that village which is beside a river. My home is there. My father's name is Ashif Khan. He is not well. I have to get medicine for him too.'

Vinay said, 'Oh, sorry! Take care of him.'

'Yes, Vinay, I always take care of him. I don't go away from him,' she said.

'Please, you can go, but please tell me who Rukhsar is,' Vinay asked.

'She is my younger sister,' she said.

Vinay said, 'She had met me in City College. You both look same.

'I had sung a song in college, this song which you sing. But on stage I forget the last line of it. Then Rukhsar had completed it. From that day, I knew that she was the girl who came in my dream. After that I searched for Rukhsar, but I never saw her again in college.'

'Yes, you are right, Vinay. We were poor that time. Please don't remind me of it. That time was not good for us. But now our good time has come. This is a blessing of God. I am realising that my bad time is over. I have got all happiness now. When will you come to my home? I will introduce you to Father,' she said.

Vinay said, 'I will definitely meet your father, but not now. Bye, Jaya Khan.'

To see Jaya made Vinay's heart weep like a child who had lost his toy. He was feeling like his destiny was going away from him. It was the same feeling for Jaya too. She was thinking that her lover was going away from her.

But he was happy that he had got his destiny. He was so impatient for her. His face was looking happy.

He went to town in his car. He brought some clothes for his mother and shoes for Payal and her favourite jalebis too. After shopping, he came back to his home.

Payal came with a smiling face to her uncle and said, 'You always take care of me.'

After dinner, Vinay's mother asked him, 'Who is Rukhsar?'

'Mother, Rukhsar is younger sister of Jaya. You know that I will never do anything wrong. You trust me, so I will maintain your trust for a lifetime.' However, he hid about Rukhsar.

Vinay asked, 'Who has informed you?'

His mother said, 'Payal told me this.'

'Oh, this is told by naughty Payal.'

Then Vinay and Payal slept close to their mother.

# 7

# Vinay Goes Home to Explain about Break-off with Tara

The next day after meeting all family members, Vinay said, 'Now I am going.'

Then mother said, 'There is a girl had who had considered you as husband. She is waiting for you. She is your best friend from childhood. Vinay, I am taking about Tara, who is your fiancée. You will not meet her?'

At first, Vinay denied, but when he remembered that mother was talking about that Tara who was friend of his childhood, then Vinay said, 'I am going there but not for meeting her. I am going to make her understand so that she forgets me. Mother, I will come at eleven o'clock, because I have to go back to my room too.'

He went to Tara's house. No one was present at Tara's house except her. Then Tara saw that Vinay is coming to meet her and she was very excited. Because her prince is coming and her dreams will come true now.

Then Vinay entered the house and met Tara.

Tara said to Vinay, 'You have quite changed, Vinay.' And she held Vinay's hand.

'You have made me wait for a long time.' Then she kept both her hands on Vinay's cheeks and said, 'I am your wife. I assumed you to be my husband because of our friendship.'

Vinay said, 'How can this be possible?

Have you gone mad?'

Then Tara said, 'Our wedding had been fixed in childhood. You should know it. I have loved you till now.'

Vinay said, 'Why are you talking like that?' I came here to break off our engagement.

Upon hearing this Tara clung to Vinay. Vinay tried to keep away from her, but she did not allow him to go.

She said, 'You are in love with Rukhsar, so you forgot me and want to go away too. Why do you love her and hate me. Am I not beautiful like her? Please accept my love. It is pure. My love is not physical. I always worship your love. I will love you very much. Whatever you like, I will do. Please don't go away from me.'

Vinay thought, 'How does she know about Rukhsar?' Then he said, 'Tara, you were not so mad like this. Why are you destroying your life because of me? See a good boy and marry him.'

On hearing this, her eyes became tearful and she said to Vinay, 'What are you saying? I haven't thought so. Still you haven't recognised my love. You don't know how much I love you.'

Vinay thought after listening to Tara's speech, 'I have made a mistake in coming here. But what is her fault? She loves me. It is not her fault. Love is gift of God, and I don't have to treat like that with Tara. It is true too that we are very good friends.' But Vinay had no reply for Tara because he loved Jaya Khan.

Vinay said to Tara, 'Now I am going, please take care of yourself, my friend.'

When Vinay started to go, she again held Vinay's hand and kissed. She said, 'I will show to the world how much I love you.'

Then Vinay said, 'Oh God, she has gone crazy in my love. Please help her.'

'You are talking to forget me. I will not forget you, neither this birth nor the next. You must come. I will be waiting.'

After Vinay left, her eyes become tearful and flowed like a river. Her face became sad as if her needs were not fulfilled. She seemed that her destiny was going away from her. She looked at him till she could see him. Then he vanished from her eyes. Then she came back to her room and went to bed. Pearls of tears dropped from her beautiful blue eyes.

Vinay went to his home. After meeting his mother, he went to his room in the city where he worked. And he started again working like before.

# 8

# Love of Lalita—I

One day, Lalita made a call on Vinay's landlord's phone. She asked, 'Please give the phone to Vinay.' Then he called Vinay and gave the phone to him.

Vinay said, 'Hello, who are you?'

'I am your friend, Lalita. I am standing at the bus stop. It's going to be night, so I cannot go home and the bus has gone too. Can I come to your room?'

For a moment, he thought, 'What should I do?' Then he remembered that she had helped him When he was in trouble

Then he replied, 'Yes, why not? You can come. I am coming there. Don't go anywhere. I am coming at the bus stop.'

Vinay didn't have a bike, so he walked to the bus stop. Lalita saw Vinay and was happy; she thought, 'My prince is coming to bring me.' Then they met. They walked back home.

Vinay said, 'We should take rickshaws.'

Then Lalita said, 'Yes, you are right.' Then they reached his room in rickshaws.

Vinay didn't talk much with Lalita. He is feeling different because of Lalita's presence in his room. He thought, 'I am doing wrong. What if my brother and mother would know that I am with a girl here? What would they think about me?' He could not talk to Lalita about what was going on with him. However, Vinay cooked food and Lalita helped too. And they slept. The room was quite silent. There was one Meter distance between them.

Once Vinay fell asleep, he dreamt of Jaya Khan, who was sister of Rukhsar and his lover of previous birth. He sang a song for her:

*Every lover like their love.*
*Sad my heart in your love.*
*When will you come back?*
*Calling to you, my lovely heart.*
*I cannot live without you*

*My heart is saying I love you.*
*I am nothing without you.*
*Someone will come in my life*
*I am waiting for my . . . lover*
*But She will never know I feeling.*
*When will I say, oh my darling?*
*It is too much; come to me soon*
*I think about you morning to noon.*
*You have to come in my heart*
*Every lover like . . .*
*My eyes searching you everywhere*
*You are my first and last desire*
*I know you will come sometime*
*My heart beating for you every time*
*We will go away from everyone*
*Every lover like . . .*

Then suddenly Lalita woke up and said, 'What are you doing?'

Then Vinay said, 'Don't stop me, Jaya. After a long day, you should understand my feeling' Vinay took Lalita in his arms and said, 'Every time you go away from me, but I will not allow you to go.' And he sinked in the love of Jaya khan. He rubbed Lalita's hair. Gradually, Lalita started liking it.

She thought, 'Vinay too loves me, like I love Vinay. Our feelings are same.' She liked Vinay's feeling and slept in the arms of Vinay.

Vinay came to know in the early morning and said, 'Oh God, she was Lalita. I have done mistake with Lalita. God, please forgive me.' Immediately, he came back to his own bed. He hated himself. He thought that it was Jaya, but she was Lalita. When they got up in the morning, then Lalita gave a smile to Vinay.

Lalita said to Vinay, 'When did you change my name from Lalita to Jaya?'

'Oh my God! Then you found out. Please forgive me. I thought that you were Jaya,' Vinay said.

'Jaya? Who is Jaya?' she asked.

'She is Rukhsar's sister. The girl whom I thought to be my dream girl was Rukhsar. But after that, I met Jaya, then found out Jaya and Rukhsar are sisters. Both are same. A song which I had sung in college, Rukhsar learnt it from her sister Jaya. In the function, I forgot the last line of the song. Then Rukhsar completed it. From that day, I thought Rukhsar is my dream girl. It seemed that she was the one I dreamt of. I think I had told you too when we had gone for my first salary at Roky Uncle's cyber cafe. The secret is open when I met Jaya. Then I found out Rukhsar is not my dream girl. She is her sister. I had told you she is my life.'

Lalita said, 'She is your life. Then what was that in the night? In the night, you played with me like a toy. What was it?'

'See, Lalita, it was my mistake that I pictured you as Jaya. If possible, then please forgive me.'

Lalita went to her home without replying to Vinay. But she was in love with Vinay. She was thinking about Vinay too much. She wanted to marry Vinay.

On the other hand, Vinay hated himself. So he made a phone call to Lalita and said, 'Please forgive me.'

Lalita said, 'I am not happy with only a sorry. You have to come to me.'

'OK, I will come to meet you. But you have to forget everything,' Vinay said.

She said, 'Why are you worried? I forgot everything. And we have not done anything wrong

Lalita became happy to hear that Vinay was ready to come. She thought again, 'Something is between us, so he phones me again and again. Vinay likes me just as I like him. Our thinking is the same.'

On the other hand, Tara loved Vinay very much too. She knew that sometime Vinay would think about their love, which was a relationship from childhood between Vinay and her. How could this pure relationship break up? But she feared that Rukhsar would take away Vinay from her.

# 9

# Jaya Khan and Rukhsar with Their Father

Both sisters, Jaya and Rukhsar, lived with their father. Their father lived at home due to an old disease. Due to less money, they couldn't study. Rukhsar loved her sister very much. They had a brother whose name was Amjad Khan. Amjad couldn't see his sisters. He was a honest and laborious man. He was like his father. When Samina Chachi used to ask him what her son would be when he grew up, then he answered to his mother that he would earn a lot of money and he would take care of his parents. Amjad's parents were very happy to see his good attitude and manners. They had believed that he would make them proud when he would grow up.

Amjad studied in the day and he went for job in the night too. His parents said to him, 'Don't do the job. This time is only for your study.' But he was not ready to accept his parents' order. One day in the evening, he got ready for his work.

He said to his parents, 'Take care yourself.'

After hearing his son's words, she said, 'I will take care of myself, but you take care yourself as night-time duty is not good for you. You are a student and you don't have to go for a job.'

Amjad's parents were thinking that was why he was saying like that.

Then he was gone for his work. His work was to load a tractor. But due to some mistake, he was run over by a tractor wheel. He was still breathing at that time, and there was no injury on his body due to the soil. But, he had internal injuries.

He said to his friend, 'You cannot save me. I have gotten hurt in the stomach.' They were going to the hospital, but on the way his breathing stopped. After post-mortem, his body was given to his parents. Amjad's parents were very depressed to see this. They lost their only son. They had only one support; he was not there now. However, they passed their time with difficulty. After a few years, two lovely babies came in their family. They kept their names Jaya and Rukhsar.

But still their fate did not change; after some time Samina Chachi died. Both sisters were too small when their mother left this world. People said to Ashif Chacha to wed again. But he did not agree to get married. Ashif Chacha not only brought them up but also taught both sisters till the tenth class. Now Ashif Chacha was not well; he was always suffering from disease. So both sisters had to face a lot of problems. Jaya had to request for help once from an aunt and once from a neighbour. Jaya knew that life tested people. She was waiting for kindness of God. She was elder to

Rukhsar. She explained to Rukhsar that Allah helped everyone. Without his permission, nothing could change in life. At Allah's house, it can be dealy, but not despair. Allah created this world for living this life with joy.

So they lived with their father, Ashif Chacha.

# 10

# Audition of Vinay

There Vinay wanted to meet Jaya. Vinay became so mad in his love that he always thought about her. But his heart said, 'First you have to get your destiny. Don't forget your first step.' Then he recalled that the next day was his audition. So he started preparing for the audition.

The next day he went for the audition with money. There he met the director. The director asked him, 'Did you bring money?'

'Yes, I have brought.'

'OK, pay there.' Then he completed his audition. He read the song of Vinay and said, 'Really, you have talent. You are selected. Start practice from tomorrow.'

The next day when the recording started, Vinay sang a song.

Then the director was happy to hear Vinay's song; he said to Vinay, 'Today I have found out how much talent you have. I hope you give me success. Our album will be a super hit in the market. I will release this album very soon if you will cooperate with me.'

In evening, Vinay went back to his room. He took some rest and thought about Jaya. After some time, Raja Bhaiya came. He said to Vinay, 'I came here to bring you with me. Vinay, please forgive me., you left home because of me. Make a promise that you will never leave home, and don't go away from Mother and our family.

Our family is not complete without you.

Vinay said, 'Don't ask for sorry. You are elder to me, and it is not good. I forgot everything about it. And you forget it too.

'I have to stay here some months. When my album will be complete, I will come home, Bhaiya. Even I don't like staying here.'

Raja Bhaiya said, 'But come home with me for some time. Mother is asking for you.'

On hearing this, his brother Vinay was ready to go home.

Vinay said to Raja Bhaiya, 'OK, let's go. I will tell Mother about me that I am selected for singing.'

Vinay had been selected for singing; he was happy that he was selected. He thought, 'Now all my dreams will be a success. Now I will explain all about me to my family.'

Then they reached home.

When Vinay met his family, his father said, 'My son, you should have come home sometime. Your mother is quite disturbed without you.'

Vinay said, 'Yes, Papa, I must come.' He touched his mother's feet. And he said, 'Mother, I have come home.'

Vinay's mother said, 'You are my son. Even after that, you live away from me. Why? Finally, what is the matter, my son?'

Then Vinay told them about his song and that he was selected for singing.

Vinay's mother said, 'It is very good, my son. You are making me proud.'

After meeting all in the family, they had a conversation about themselves.

Then Vinay said to his mother, 'Payal told you about Rukhsar. That is not right. Actually Rukhsar is her sister. When I met Jaya, then I found out she is her sister. Since childhood the girl that I dreamt about is Jaya. She is living with her family near our village.'

'My son, she belongs to another religion's family. You know this. Even after that, you are saying you love her.'

'Yes, Mother . . .'

They were talking when in between Payal came and said, 'Uncle, what did you bring for me?'

'I brought for you jalebi.' Then Vinay and his family had dinner. After having dinner, his mother and Payal had some conversation again and then went to sleep.

# 11

## Vinay Goes to Jaya Khan's Auntie's Village to Meet Her

The next day, Vinay went to Jaya's village to meet her. He didn't know her house, so he asked the villagers, 'Where is the house of Jaya Khan, She is the sister of Rukhsar'

The villager asked Vinay, 'Who are you?'

Vinay replied to them, 'My name is Vinay.'

'What is she to you and why do you want to meet her?'

Vinay was about to reply to the people when Rukhsar came and recognised him. She said to Vinay, 'You are asking for Jaya, right? Come with me.'

Rukhsar and Vinay had already met in college.

She said to Vinay, 'Come with me to my home.'

They reached Jaya's home, with Vinay and Rukhsar talking to each other. But Vinay thought, 'Where is Jaya?'

'She is busy in some work so she is not visible.'

Rukhsar said to Vinay, 'In college, you sang a song of my sister and forgot the last line of that song. Then I completed the song that time, do you remember?'

'Yes, Rukhsar, I remember it. Even Payal was there. She asked me about you.'

'Then why didn't you bring her with you?'

Vinay's eyes searched for Jaya while he talked with Rukhsar. Finally he asked where Jaya was.

Rukhsar replied, 'She has gone to aunt's (her mother's sister) village.'

On hearing this, his face became sad, like someone had slapped him. His happiness of five days to see his lover changed in disunion.

Then she introduced Vinay to her father.

'Father, this is Vinay Shrivastav, son of Dilip Shrivastav. He studies in City College.'

Ashif Chacha said, 'Oh, you are son of Dilip. How is your business going on?'

'I don't know about the business. But everything is fine.'

He asked her father why Jaya went to the old well which was near the temple. 'Do you know it? Even you belong to another religion, but you haven't refused to go there.'

'Vinay, she used to say that her lover Mohit had been killed there by enemy of their love. So she go to there to wait for him. She also used to say that Mohit was her lover of her dream. They played there. And she worshipped God in that temple. But some people killed her lover.'

Vinay asked Jaya's father, 'And you believe this?'

'Yes, Vinay, some people have been able to remember their previous birth memory. Jaya is one of them.

Then Vinay said to Jaya's father, 'One day, Jaya and I met in that temple. She told me that I was her Mohit. And even I used to dream of her also since childhood.'

'Oh, so you are Mohit! I was thinking too. That was why this boy came here. Not only your speech but also your eyes are saying that you are searching for someone. I am sure that you are Mohit. Jaya wanted to meet you too. Would you like to meet her?'

'Yes, I want to meet her. Please tell me how can I meet her.'

Then Jaya's father said, 'Rukhsar will take you to her aunt's house where she is.'

Then Vinay started the car and they departed from there. On the way, she explained to Vinay, 'If someone asks you your name, then speak to him with confidence and say, "I am Aslam." And don't talk too much.'

After some time, they crossed the flyover over the river and they reached Rukhsar's aunt's village.

Then she said to Jaya, 'See, Jaya, who has come. Your lover!

Their aunt asked Rukhsar who was he.

She said to their aunt, 'He is the son of Khan Baba and come to meet Jaya.'

Then their aunt asked to Vinay, 'How is Khan baba? I haven't seen him for a long time. What is the matter?'

'Actually, Aunt, he is quite busy in business out of the country. Even he will meet us after a long time.'

'OK, stay here tonight. We are offering goat to almighty. Today is the day of blood. We have invited our relatives too on this great occasion.'

As he listened to her aunt, Vinay got nervous. His heart started beating fast. Now his intention was changed regarding meeting with Jaya. He thought, 'Where I came, oh Mom?'

But he didn't say anything; otherwise they would know who he was.

Then Vinay called Jaya to a separate place and said to her, 'I am not feeling well here.'

'Let's go somewhere.'

Jaya took permission from her aunt that they were going on to their field.

Then Vinay and Jaya reached the field and sat for some time. The entire field looked green and cool wind was blowing. On seeing this wonderful scene's natural beauty, they felt good. The heart of Vinay was now in control.

But he could not forget it; he asked Jaya, 'Why do people offer life of animals to almighty? If this is religion then how would be nonreligion. They were killing animals who can not speak. But oh God forgive them they don't know what they are doing. Almighty will never like to take life of someone because he created life of all, even that of animals too and almighty has given right to every creature to live life without boundation 'almighty understand only feeling, wish, desire not taste, money or life of animal.

'Vinay, you are right. The meaning of immolate is sacrifice (leave) our evil. I mean, we all have to leave all bad habits like ego, dishonesty, misbehaviour. We have to help the physically challenged people and start our life with new thinking from this day. Our religion is great because many moral teachings are given by Mohamed Sahib, like we have to live this life not for ourselves but live this life for others.

'Give affection to all. Altruistic love is best immolation for God. Benevolence for all is immolation for God. We should all pray to Allah for this world and all religions so that all people can understand and change their misbehaviour with religion. Religion is always holy and we all have to respect it by heart'

Vinay said, 'Today I understand what religion is. I came here after meeting your father. He is a very good person. He did not stop you from going to the temple, even though you belong to a different religion.'

'Yes, Vinay, he always trusts me. And I always obey the orders of him too.'

'This is very good thinking and understanding in your family,' said Vinay.

Now he came to close Jaya and held her hand. 'I was dying to meet you, but when I heard about the offering all my feelings changed. And you are really so wise and intelligent. I know this today.'

Jaya said, 'I had to wait for you for many years. I knew that you will come definitely.'

Vinay said, 'I love you so much. You don't know this but my wedding was fixed with Tara by my family. But I have broken up with my fiancée now because I like you. I think (remember) only about you since you called me at that temple and sang a song. I concede you to be my princess. My fiancée Tara loves me too much. She concedes (assumes) me to be her husband. I want that she forgets me.'

'Your fiancée?'

'Yes, Jaya, it is right. My wedding was fixed in childhood with Tara.'

'You don't worry, Vinay. Allah will help us.'

'Jaya, I would like to become a singer. After that I will marry you. You will wait for me?'

'I have only been waiting till now and will wait until I will find you.'

Vinay said to Jaya, 'I will drop you at your aunt's home, then I will go to my house. My director was asking for me. I came here without informing him.'

Then he came back to his house.

The next day after meeting his family, Vinay went to the studio.

His director said, 'Vinay, where had you gone? You don't have any number so I can call you. Take this mobile. You keep it always with you. Whenever I need you, I will call you on your mobile.'

'Thank you, sir. Please forgive me for whatever is pending due to me. I will take care next time.'

'There is no need for sorry, but you have to start your pending work with a full heart from today. After five songs are completed our album will be complete, but Vinay, what is the name of this album?'

'This album's name is *Lover of Previous Birth*.'

'Oh, lover of previous birth. What a name! How did you think about it?'

'Sir, I will tell you this later.'

# 12

## Love of Lalita – II

From the studio, he came back to his room. He was surprised to see Lalita in his room. He said, 'When did you come?'

She replied, 'Just now. My bus has gone, so I came here. It is not good to go home so late. If you have any problem, then I can go, even in night.'

'No, not a problem, but you should come after informing me. At least you should call me. It is not good to stay in my room. If my family finds out about it, then what will they think about me? And if my lover Jaya will know, then she will never tolerate this.'

'OK, dear, I am going. Due to me, my dearest will face disrepute. But in the night I will be spooked, then what shall I do?'

Then Vinay said, 'OK, don't go today. You stay, but next time whenever you come please inform.'

After having dinner, they went to sleep. In the night, Lalita put an arm around Vinay from the back and kissed Vinay. After that, she fell asleep, with her arm around Vinay. In the morning, he found that she had put her arm around him. Then he said to Lalita, 'Have you gone crazy? What are you doing?'

She woke up and said to Vinay, 'I am sorry. I thought you are my boyfriend. So I made this mistake.'

'Lalita, I know you are taking revenge against me for that day,' said Vinay.

'No, no, Vinay, it is not true,' she replied.

'But it is not good for me. My love is meant for someone else.'

'Yes, Vinay, I put my hand on your honour. My heart is saying to cut my hands,' she said.

'OK, OK, don't make a speech. Leave in the morning. My brother is coming tomorrow.'

'OK, Vinay,' she said.

Vinay helped Lalita to board the bus at the bus stop in the morning. She became sad as she was going away from her love.

'Bye, see you again,' she said.

After some time, he came back to his room and went to the bathroom to have a bath. His elder brother, Raja, and Payal come. Raja asked the landowner where Vinay was.

'Maybe he is in the bathroom. So you are his brother?'

'Yes, I am his elder brother, Raja.'

'OK, tell me one thing. A girl came here two times, and she said that she is fiancée of Vinay. Is it true?' he asked Raja.

'Yes, it is true. She is his fiancée from childhood. My brother's wedding is fixed with her. Don't have misapprehension about my brother. He is a very simple and kind man.'

Then Vinay came and said, 'Bhaiya, when did you come?'

'I have just come. How are you?'

'I am fine, Bhaiya, and you?'

'I am fine too.'

'I'll make tea, Bhaiya.'

'No, Vinay, don't make tea. I am in a hurry. Come with us. Mother has called you.'

'I cannot come home for two more days. I have urgent work in the studio. Even my boss will not allow me. I will come after two days. Leave Payal here. We will come together.'

'She will disturb you.'

'No, Brother, I will manage,' replied Vinay.

'As you wish,' Raja said.

Payal was glad to meet Vinay because he helped her in her studies. And he also gave her jalebi and chocolate too.

Payal said, 'Uncle, I cannot seem to do well without you, even I don't like to study. Papa does not teach me.'

'You don't worry about it. I will teach you.'

Vinay took Payal to his studio.

His boss asked Vinay, 'Who is she?'

'She is my niece.' His boss said oh good!

Then his boss introduced Payal to Rahul. Rahul is his ten-year-old son. Then they both played together while the studio work was in progress.

Vinay's boss said to him, 'Today there is a lot of work. So let's start pending work with full effort. Today we have to complete two songs.'

Then music started.

On listening to this good song, his team and boss were happy; they said, 'This song is very good.'

Vinay did his job with full effort. He completed his work and he went back his room in the evening. Then he cooked food.

Payal looked at Vinay and thought, 'Uncle does a lot of effort, then why did he leave home?'

They had dinner and went to bed.

The next day he went to office as usual and did a lot of effort like the day before. He knew that if we didn't work by heart we would never be successful.

After his two songs were complete, they both came back to the room.

The next day, they went home. First he touched his mother's feet. 'I will be a singer because of your blessings. Whatever I am today, it is due to you. My album is going to be complete. Give me blessings so that I will get my destiny.'

Then his mother said, 'I am seeing the desire of destiny in your eyes. Your aim is only to get your destiny. You will get your destiny very soon, my son. Don't worry, my blessing is always with you.'

'Mother, I wanted to hear these words. After listening to this, all my wishes are complete. I wanted to touch your feet.'

Then his mother said, my own son don't like me as you like me Vinay. You believe in me and listen to me carefully and always follow me.'

Vinay said, this is my duty. Then they talked to each other. After some time, his mother said, 'Take a rest. You seem tired.'

Then he went to bed in the night. He had a dream that Jaya was calling him. But some people didn't allow her to go to him. Even he tried to meet her. A man hit Vinay's head with an iron rod. He woke up and became nervous. There was sweat on his head.

Whenever he would get such a bad dream, he would go to his mother and sleep there. So he did the same; he went to his mother and slept there.

The next day he got up and thought about that dream and why he got such a bad dream. Then he said to his mother, 'I have to go Jaya's village to meet her.'

'Go, my son. When have I ever denied you from going somewhere?'

His mother thought, 'That girl has done magic on my son. He doesn't go anywhere before time, but now he is changed due to her. God, save my child. Help my son.'

# 13

# Jaya and Rukhsar Become Orphans

Vinay went to Jaya's house to meet her. When he reached there, he saw that a large crowd had gathered near Jaya's house. He became nervous on seeing that. 'What has happened?' he thought. 'Perhaps somebody has passed away.' Then somebody told Vinay that Jaya's father had died. Vinay become unhappy on hearing that. His eyes became tearful. He thought that both sisters had now become orphans. They had only one support, and now he was gone. Now who would help them? Then Vinay saw both Jaya and Rukhsar, who were weeping bitterly.

Vinay went to Jaya and said to her, 'Jaya, this life takes a test of everyone. This is the wish of God. Nobody can change it. Today you have lot of grief, but one day God will rain happiness on your family.'

On listening to these words, people said, 'Very good, gentleman. You are right.'

Vinay said, 'Live this life with full of joy. Your problem will be solved automatically.' For this you have to only trust on almighty, who is managing this world.

Then they decorated the bier of Ashif Chacha with flowers. Ashif Chacha was buried at twelve o'clock. It was the mourning time. Vinay stayed there that night.

When Vinay went away, Anjum Sheikh asked Jaya, 'Who is that boy that was talking to you yesterday?'

Then Jaya said, 'He is the son of my father's friend. They helped us very much when Mother was suffering from disease.'

So saying she put off his questions. But he had found out about him the day Jaya and Vinay had gone to her aunt's field. Jaya and Vinay were roistering in the field.

After Ashif Chacha's death, Anjum's eyes fell on Jaya. He wanted to wed Jaya. But Jaya hadn't given any indication to Anjum. He knew that she liked that boy. He was jealous of Vinay.

He went to Vinay and asked him, 'What is your name?'

Vinay answered with confidence, 'I am Aslam

'I know you are not a local, then from where do you belong after all?'

They were talking when Vinay got a call from his home. His mother said, 'Where are you staying without informing me? I have been waiting since yesterday and your phone is switched off too.'

'Mother, I will tell you everything.' He got into the car while talking with his mother. Then he started the car and departed for home. Anjum saw that Aslam was in such a hurry and so couldn't even reply to him.

# 14

## Tara and Vinay Meet Again

Vinay was coming home, but on the way Tara recognised Vinay's. Then she cried out loudly, 'Vinay, I am your fiancée. Stop the car.'

There was a lot of crowd so he was driving at twenty to thirty miles per hour. He heard Tara's voice, but he didn't stop the car. Then Tara became angry and said, 'You come after meeting that witch. I know what else you can do. You are a playboy.'

Then he stopped the car and came back to Tara; he said to Tara, 'Have you gone mad? If you don't know about something, then you should think before speaking. Her father is no more and you are talking such nonsense. You have really gone crazy. You don't know about her.'

'Please forgive me. I didn't know that. But whenever that girl meets you I don't like it. I would like to kill. Whoever comes between our love and i am ready to fight every trouble that will come in our love's way.

Vinay thought, 'What should I reply to her?'

Then she said, 'Why didn't you stop when I was calling you?'

Vinay said, 'I got a call from home to come soon. And I am quite late. I have to go to office too after leaving this car at home.'

'You worry about office so much, then why did you come here? Why don't you stay in office forever?'

When he heard this, he couldn't reply. As Vinay was speechless, she understood that Vinay had accepted his mistake.

'OK, come to my home and stay for some time, then you can go home.'

Vinay replied, 'I cannot come at any cost.'

She became sad and said, 'Swear on our childhood relationship you have to come.'

Then Vinay remembered, 'We were younger and that time our friendship was very close, and today she swore on that relationship. She thinks that I should go with her.' So he was ready to go to Tara's house.

Tara said, 'You made me wait for a long time. Let's go. At home, my parents want to meet you, so meet them too.'

Then they reached her home; as soon as they entered Tara's home, her father said, 'There is no need to bring him here. He is a cheater, you don't know, Tara? I found out from his landlord that a girl came to his room and she introduced herself as fiancée of Vinay and stayed with him two times in his room. Would you love Vinay still?'

On hearing this, she lost consciousness and fell down on the ground. Her head collided with the table. Due to this injury, little bit of blood came on her head. Then her father rushed to her and lifted her and laid her on the bed. Vinay called the doctor immediately. After some time, the doctor came. He said after checking, 'Don't worry. It is an ordinary injury. She will be all right.'

After some time, she became conscious. Vinay rubbed her hair and said, 'I am not a good friend. I don't love you, even though you love me very much. Why?'

Tara said, 'I am thirsty for your love, Vinay. You pat my head. It seems I have got all the happiness of world in my life.'

Vinay said this to Tara to raise hate in his heart for her because he doesn't like the fact that Tara loves him. But she didn't understand what Vinay wanted.

She said, 'You take me in your arms like this. I want to live in your arms. I am ready to face any accident such as this just to live your arms. Please keep me always with you. Don't leave me.'

'OK, now take rest. You don't know you fell down on the ground before,' Vinay said.

Tara said, 'I will follow you. I will accept your every law. I want you and I want to live with you as you want. But you sit with me. Stay in front of me. Do not go away.'

On listening to Tara speak like this, her father thought, 'My daughter has gone love mad in his love. And he is a cheater.'

Vinay kept his hand on her head, and she fell asleep. Then Vinay said, 'I am going, Uncle. Take care of her.'

After this, her father's hatred was no less; he said, 'You are a cheater and will never improve.'

Vinay said, 'If possible, please forgive me.' Then he departed from there after saying these words. He went back home. He said to his mother, 'Jaya's father is no more. Go and meet her. My boss is calling me, so I am in a hurry.'

When he reached his studio, he said, 'I am sorry.' Vinay explained to his boss the reason for coming late.

'Don't worry, my son. You are a responsible man. Come on time from tomorrow.' Then music started.

Vinay thought about Jaya and sang a song:

*My sweetheart, my beloved.*
*I cannot live without you.*
*This heart fell into your love.*
*I cannot suffer this pain of love!*
*You are my first and last love.*
*You called me Mohit with love.*
*You always live in my breath.*
*You keep me in your eyes.*
*It was no.*
*My sweetheart, my beloved.*
*I cannot live without you!*
*Why you trouble me in my dream?*
*Why you made me weep in disunion?*
*I won't go away from you.*
*I can be some story my heart says.*
*And this is August month now.*
*My sweetheart, my beloved.*
*I cannot live without you!*

After listening to this song, the director became happy and embraced Vinay. 'Very good, you sing well. One day, you will make me proud. But don't forget us.'

'No, sir, I will always remember you. This all is given by you only. Without you, I am nothing, sir.'

'One more song is remaining. After that, we will launch our album.'

Vinay became happy to hear that his album was coming in the market for the first time. He thought, 'Now my destiny is coming to me.' He had full confidence. 'Work which is done by full heart definitely brings success in life. I have to carry on getting closer to my destiny.'

# 15

## Tara's Jealousy with Jaya Khan

Tara is jealous of Jaya and Vinay's love. She was quite disturbed with her. She couldn't tolerate this. She started her car and went to Jaya's home. She knew that it was not good to talk in front of her sister, so she called her to a lonely place.

She said to Jaya, 'I request you to please don't come between Vinay and me. Please go away from Vinay and me. I found out it that you went to Vinay's room and stayed there, even in the night. Now I cannot tolerate this. It is too much now. This is not a pardonable mistake. Whatever you want take from me but leave my lover Vinay.'

After listening to this virulent speech, Jaya lost her head. 'And she said who said I went to meet Vinay in his room and stay there? You have lost your senses and are saying this unbelievable story.'

Then Tara said, 'My father has found this from Vinay's landlord. He was telling to my father that the fiancée of Vinay went there two times.'

'Ms Tara, you don't know. I have loved Mohit, who has been my valentine since my previous birth.'

'Then why go love mad after my Vinay?'

Then Jaya explained the entire story. 'We are both separated lovers since our previous birth and waiting for each other. My name was Shivangini and I loved Mohit. But people hadn't like our love. Even our family did not like our love. They took away my love from me, and I came here searching for him in this birth. I am waiting for our meeting.'

Tara thought, 'Perhaps this is a true story.' Now she knew the reality.

Then Tara said, 'You are taking away my love from me who is my lover.'

Jaya said, 'You are taking away my Mohit from me, as I have already been waiting since many years. And you are disturbing me. This is not fair.'

Tara said finally, 'Who is the third person who was going to Vinay's room and coming in our way of our love? We have to find out.'

Jaya said, 'Vinay loves only me and I love him very much.'

'You are right, but who knows what he is doing there? Even he didn't inform you about his misdeed?'

After this, Tara became sad and went back to her home. She came to know that Rukhsar was sister of Jaya. And she understood that Jaya was her love's enemy. But Vinay loved Jaya, not Rukhsar. Now Tara clearly saw that her love's destiny was going away from her.

And that side, Vinay was thinking about Jaya. He wanted to live with Jaya, but his album was not complete. 'How I will get time to meet her?' He got happiness from two sides: one was that his album was going to be complete and another was he was thinking about Jaya Khan and that their day of meeting was coming soon.

Then his friend who worked with him asked him, 'What is the matter? Why are you so happy today? Tell us. Share your secrets of happiness with us, dear.'

Vinay lied and said, 'This happiness is our success. By all our efforts, we are going to launch our album. Thanks to all for cooperating with each other and doing a great job.'

Then one girl whose name was Saneha Rajpoot asked Vinay, 'To whom do you dedicate this song, how have you written this song? Perhaps you have a lover or a special someone?'

Then Vinay laughed and said, 'She is Jaya Khan. She is my lover.'

Then Vinay's team said, 'Oh, your love is so true that you became a singer.' They all laughed.

Then Vinay's boss said, 'This album will be a super hit in the market.'

Vinay said, 'You have given me a chance to come up. Thanks for this. This album is a result of your effort.'

Vinay thought about his mother, 'I need my mother's blessings to make this album a success. Then this album will definitely be a success. This will be complete tomorrow, and I have to go home too.' Then Vinay made a call to his mother. He said to his mother, 'How are you?'

'I am fine,' 'But when will you come back?' his mother said.

'I am coming tomorrow. Give me blessings so that my work will be a success.'

'My blessing is always with you. Take care of yourself.'

He went back to his room after talking to his mother.

# 16

# Love of Lalita — III:
# Last Long Meeting with Vinay

He went back to his room and rested; in the meanwhile, he got a call of Lalita.

'Hi.'

'I miss you, I kiss you, I love you, and how are you, tell me?

Vinay reply Don't time pass with me? I am already busy How was my poetry?' said Lalita.

'Not good. By the way, how are you?' asked Vinay.

'How am I? I am standing the bus stop. Come and fetch me.'

Then Vinay said, 'Why don't you come in the day? Every time you come late and come to me. I am already infamous because of you.'

Lalita laughed at this sentence. 'And she said even if you say you don't love me it doesn't matter. Maybe it is written in my fate so. I am only infamous because of your name, not your love in my fate.'

'Stop passing time and listen to me carefully. The landlord has told to my brother.'

'So what have we done wrong?' I only stayed in your room to pass the night and it was already late, said Lalita.

'Please understand me,' said Vinay, but she disconnected the call. Then he felt that he had done a mistake to say such virulent words. 'That time when we didn't even know each other, she had given my bail. And today I give her such a virulent speech. God, please forgive me and save me from such faith problem. If she has gone home on such a night and something happens in the way, then I will be responsible for this.'

He went to the bus stop to bring her. Then he searched for her here and there, but she couldn't be seen. He became nervous and thought that if she faced any problem on the way then who would help her. He held his head and thought, 'What I have done?' Then he cried loudly, 'Lalita, where are you? I came to take you.' For some time, he regretted, 'How can she have gone? I was just saying to her simply. How will she go in such a night?' He got angry at himself. 'What have I done?'

One more time, he cried loudly, 'Lalita, I came to take you with me.' At the bus stop, everybody became silent after listening to Vinay's voice.

All eyes were on him. A media reporter was also there with the camera; he started shooting Vinay and asked him, 'Whom are you searching for?'

'Why are you so sad?' Vinay's attention was on Lalita, not on the camera, so he didn't reply to him. In the meantime, Lalita came fast and embraced Vinay. Now she felt that Vinay loved her very much and could not live without her.

At this time, after he found her, he was so happy that he wasn't aware she had embraced him and the camera captured him like a film shooting.

Everybody who saw this started clapping. They said, 'Now you got whom you were searching. You were searching for her, right?'

'Thank God, I got her, otherwise how could she go home so late?'

After some time, they came to his room. Lalita realised that Vinay looked tired. So she said to him, 'You take rest. I will cook food.'

Then she cooked food. Vinay said, 'Yes, you understand me. I am really tired today.' And he thanked her.

She said to herself, 'Now time is coming that you have to understand my feelings.'

After some time, Vinay wanted to go to sleep. He knew that Lalita would disturb him, so he left the entire bed for her so that he could sleep properly. He went to the kitchen with a bed sheet and carpet for sleeping. He spread the mat on the floor. He fell asleep. But after some time, Lalita came there. She put an arm around Vinay from the back.

Vinay said to her, 'What are you doing? Why did you come here? Leave me and please go to your bed.'

She said, 'I am afraid and I cannot sleep alone.'

'So why are you taking me in your arms? You don't know I love Jaya Khan.'

Then they were sleeping facing the opposite side of each other. But even then she wasn't able to sleep. She turned to Vinay's side and kissed him. Vinay tried to make her understand many times, but she didn't listen.

She said, 'I know you love me very much, but you cannot express it to me. If you didn't like, then why were you disturbed for me at the bus stop? And you didn't oppose me when I embraced you in front of all.'

'Have you gone mad? Why don't you understand me? That time I was disturbed due to you. It is right because you are my friend. And that time I forgot and didn't know what had happened. I didn't have sense because I was excited that time to find you. Stop thinking about me. I am only for my lover.'

Then she moved on to his chest and kissed him on his lips. Vinay got angry by this misdeed of Lalita. He slapped her on her face. Her fair face became red.

She went to a corner and started weeping. Vinay was afraid that if somebody heard the voice of Lalita then what would they think.

He said, 'Please stop weeping. What will people think about me?' But she did not listen and continued weeping. 'Please forgive me. I will never slap you.' Still she continued to weep. Then finally he said, 'Do as you wish but stop crying, Lalita.' Still Lalita didn't react. She wanted to see Vinay writhe in pain.

That made Vinay angry and he said, 'Lalita, what kind of problem are you?' He kissed Lalita on her lips until her weeping stopped. Finally, he took her in his arms and slept. But Vinay's soul was saying, 'You are not being fair. Your lover is waiting for you and you are embracing someone else.' But he was helpless.

In the night, he wanted to leave her and go away. But she said loudly, 'Never go away from me.'

Then he slept again there, although he couldn't sleep properly that night.

He got up in the morning. He said to her, 'Lalita, I will drop you at the bus stop. I have to go to office.'

'You too comeing home today so we can go together.'lalita said

'No, Lalita, if I will come with you, then what will people think about me? And I don't want to come with you too. In the night, you had stopped my breath. I was quite disturbed by you.

Then she realised that what she did with Vinay was wrong.

She said, 'Please forgive me.'

Vinay didn't reply, but after a moment he said, 'I will go home in the evening, not now. In the office, a lot of work is pending, so I will be late. You can go.'

Lalita said, 'Why do you fear about people? We will go together so that we will not feel bored on the way. And you love me and fear too.'

'Who said I love you? I love only Jaya Khan, not you.'

'Then why couldn't you see me weeping in the night? I know you cannot see me sad, because you love me very much. Say it is right.'

'I love Jaya Khan only, not you. I have explained more than one time to you.'

She thought, 'He was searching me, so he was fidgeting with tension at the bus stop, and after finding me, he was so happy that he didn't know that I had taken him in my arms. It means he definitely loves me.'

'I know you love me. You fear to say only, nothing else.'

'Lalita, still you don't have any sense and do not understand. Last night, I was afraid that if people heard your voice, then what would they think? So I had to do all that.'

'So do you really not love me, Vinay?'

'Yes, Lalita, now you understand me. I love Jaya Khan only. I won't live without her.'

On hearing these words, her blue eyes became tearful. Her heart was crying from inside. Her face became sad. Vinay could not see her look sad; he could not stop this emotion. He thought, 'Her heart will break if she will not get me.' So he said, 'OK, we will go home together. But I have to go to my office too. You wait for me at the bus stop. Then I will drop you at your home.'

After this, Vinay went to his office and Lalita went to her uncle's home.

Vinay met everyone in the office. Vinay's boss said to him, 'Today is the last day of completion of the album and then we will take rest. Now we will get our fruit of labour.' So we have to work by heart. Then they start his job.

Vinay thought, now my album is going to be complete.'

Vinay thanked all. After that, he touched the director's feet. His boss was impressed by his great work, and he embraced Vinay. He said, 'You are lucky for me. After your coming, all my incomplete work has got complete now.'

Vinay said, 'You have given me a chance to come up too.' They talked to each other, after conversation Vinay went back to his room, because he had given time to Lalita to go home together. He was ready to go home.

He reached the bus stand. She was waiting for him. She was happy to see Vinay.

'Come in time. Sometimes I have noticed you are always late.'

'Today is my last day of completing my album. So I am late.

They both sat in the bus and the bus departed from the bus stand. On the way she said, 'I am going to sleep. You know that I couldn't sleep last night. Can I put my head on your shoulder?'

'OK, you can.'

He said to himself angrily 'Not only put your head but also all the people who are in the bus. My shoulder is public property. Why did I bring her with me, and I am undergo all her demands.'

After some time, Vinay said, 'You don't believe me. I will introduce you to Jaya Khan.'

On hearing Jaya's name, her heart started beating fast. She thought, 'Now Vinay is going to go away.'

Vinay got the bus to stop, and they got down. She asked nervously, 'Why have we got down here?'

'We will meet Jaya Khan. She comes here, so that you can believe me.'

They went towards the temple. They reached the temple and Vinay explained to her about his lover. He waited for Jaya. He shouted loudly, 'Jaya, I am Mohit come to see you. Where are you?' There was no reply for Vinay. He waited for a long time, but no one came there. Vinay said, 'I think she is not coming because of you.' Then they were ready to go.

Then they heard a song:

*Forget me, my lover*
*Don't call me however*
*You were my love*
*Support of my love.*
*But you deceive me*
*This is not pardonable*
*Don't call me however*
*Forget me, my lover . . . !*
*I have waited birth after birth.*
*You are not my love lever*
*Why I remember i forget everything*
*Forget me, my lover . . . !*
*I am burning in your love*
*I am melting fire of love*
*Forget me, don't call now*
*Forget me, my lover . . . !*

Then they saw that she was leaving. Vinay called her, 'Please stop, my sweetheart.'

'For God's sake, don't stop me. I can't bear that you are with someone else.'

Then Lalita said, 'See, Jaya, I don't know you, but I know this that Vinay loves you very much. He saves all his feelings only for you. You have misunderstood.'

But she did not stop and went without replying. She was crying inside.

It was the same here with Vinay, who had become sad too.

Lalita said, 'All this has happened due to me. Please forgive me. Your love has been destroyed by me.' She was regretful. She said, 'Vinay, if possible please forgive me. You were right. I should have not met you.'

Don't worry. It is my fate, so it is done by God.this is not your fault. So don't feel guilty.'

# 17

# Vinay at Lalita's House

Vinay said Lalita OK, now let's go. I will help you board the bus to go to your home.'

She said, 'Please give me your phone.' She made a call to her brother, Tanuj Shrivastav. She called him at Menasha dhaba (road hotel).

While Tanuj was coming to Menasha dhaba, they went to the dhaba (road hotel) and sat on the chairs. Lalita was looking upset; she thought, 'This is the last long-time meeting with Vinay.' She said to herself, 'if vinay will marry me than my life become really injoyful. But my fate is not with me. He is not in my life. Lucky Is who whom he likes.'

Then Vinay asked, 'Oh, where are you? What are you thinking so deep?'

'Nothing, I am thinking about my love.'

After some time, Tanuj came and said, 'Lalita Didi (sister), what are you doing here? I am waiting for you the last two days and you now call me here.'

'Sorry, Tanuj, actually I was busy I couldn't call you.'

'Don't worry. Now I have come.'

After seeing Vinay, Tanuj said, 'Didi (sister), I have seen this man on television. He is a great man, you don't know. He is a singer.'

Then Lalita came to knew that Vinay is a singer.

Lalita was so love mad after Vinay that she didn't know that Vinay was a singer and he was working at music studio. Then she remembered that in college Vinay had given a warning to that boys, 'One day my song will come in the market.' It was right.

Vinay said, 'Now, let's go.'

Then they sat in the car to leave from there. Then Tanuj said, 'Please come to my home, Mr Vinay sir.'

Vinay said, 'I cannot come now.'

Lalita said, 'Why don't you come to my home? I have come to your home many times, then why don't you come to my home? What is the problem? If you will not come to my home, I will consider that you don't think about others. You think about yourself, like a selfish person.'

'OK, you don't need to say this speech. I am coming with you.'

On hearing this, she was happy from inside.

Lalita's home was in a very good area of the city. Her house was quite big, but they were only two of them, so they must feel lonely. Except a maid no one else lived in that big house. Even Vinay hadn't seen her house. She neither told Vinay nor showed her house and family.

Then Vinay asked Tanuj, 'Are your parents living there with you?'

He replied, 'No, my father is a civil engineer in Assam. And my mother passed away ten years before.'

'Oh, sorry!'

He became unhappy to know that Lalita lost her mother, love of mother is not in her fate. She was living with her brother.

Lalita said, 'Tanuj, call the maid so that she will cook our food. I am very hungry, brother.'

He replied, 'You call her. I am busy and I don't have her number.'

'My brother, please call her and I don't have her number too.' They argued with each other.

Finally Vinay said, 'Can I make a call to the maid for cooking food?'

Tanuj said, 'No, sir, I will call her. I have her mobile number, but you don't know. Didi (sister) is very lazy.' Tanuj called her, and said 'Please cook food for us. We are coming.'

After some time, they reached home. Vinay and Lalita got off the car. Tanuj went to park the car in the car parking area. Lalita was happy to see Vinay at her home for the first time. In that happiness, she held Vinay's hand and said, 'Come into my home.'

'Lalita, what are doing?'

She let go of his hand immediately. Then they entered her home. After freshening up, they had dinner after this Vinay and Tanuj had a conversation in Tanuj's study. Vinay asked Tanuj, 'In which college are you studying?'

Tanuj explained to Vinay, 'I am a second year IT student in NITM College, Gwalior.' He also said to Vinay, 'I am a fan of yours. Many times I have seen you in interviews.'

Vinay said, 'You should study well. Don't leave your destiny's way. You will definitely succeed.'

'Don't forget me when you become a great singer. My exam is starting from third December, so I going to my study room. The maid has arranged your bed in the guest room. If you don't fall asleep then watch television, even after you feel bore then come to me.'

Then Tanuj went to his study room. Lalita knew that Vinay would definitely come to the guest room. So she went there and waited for Vinay. When Vinay reached the guest room, he saw Lalita was there too. He became nervous and thought, 'If Tanuj comes to know about us, what will he think about me? She will make my image zero in front of Tanuj.'

Vinay said, 'Please go from here. If Tanuj finds about this, he will feel very bad. Lalita, please understand.'

Lalita said, 'Don't worry. He doesn't come this side.'

'Vinay said If you stay here in this room, then I will go from this room, Lalita.'

On hearing this, she became sad.

Then Vinay remembered that she didn't have her mother and he was making her unhappy. Then he came and sat on the bed. He said, 'OK, Lalita, sit for some time. You can go later.'

On hearing this, she became a little happy.

Vinay switched on the TV, but she said, 'I don't like TV this time.' Then he switched off the TV and covered himself with a quilt.

She didn't like this; she said, 'Come, Vinay, i want to talk to you about something.'

Vinay replied, 'I am going to sleep. You too, go and sleep. It is so late.'

Lalita said, 'I am sitting here waiting for you and you switched the TV off because you want to sleep and now you are telling me to go and sleep in my room. What is this, Vinay? You are so insensitive that you don't know if someone wants to be with you and you don't even understand my feeling. I am going on and on here, and are you even listening to me?'

Then Vinay said, 'What do you want to say, Lalita?'

'I want to come in your quilt and want to sleep in your arms.'

'Lalita, what are you saying? You don't know my lover is waiting for me. I will never deceive her. I saved my love only for her. My feelings are so pure that it will never do wrong.'

Lalita couldn't reply to Vinay. She became silent, but she tried to put an arm around Vinay. He opposed her, but she didn't stop. Vinay knew she was very stubborn. Stopping her meant hitting head against a stone.

But Lalita's love was not physical. After seeing Lalita's feelings, he prayed to God, 'Please give her such a husband who will love her very much and who will take care of her forever.' Then he remembered that his classmate Archit liked Lalita very much. 'I should talk with him.' After this, he fell asleep. Lalita took him in her arms and slept. They both fell asleep.

In the morning, he woke up to find that she had put an arm around him. He tried to move away from her. But she woke up and said, 'Jaya Khan has won you, but I can't win your heart. Why?'

To that Vinay didn't reply.

She said again, 'Any moment of life, whenever you need me call me. I will be there. My heart is always open for your love till the last breath.'

On listen to this, his heart became quite heavy with grief. He was helpless and prayed for her to God.

He was waiting silently for sunrise. As morning was approaching, her sadness was increasing because with sunrise she would go away from Vinay. She was thinking, 'This is the last big meeting with my sweetheart.'

Vinay said, 'Wake up, Lalita. It is morning time. Even Tanuj has woken up.'

She got up and asked the maid to get tea.

In the morning, Vinay went to Tanuj and said, 'Please drop me.' But he found that he was very busy, so he said, 'OK, don't worry. Carry on. I will go myself.'

'Sorry, I was busy. I will drop you at your home.' Lalita heard this; she too needed a chance to go with Vinay.

So she said, 'You pay attention to your studies. I will drop Vinay at his home.'

Then they sat in the car. Tanuj vale Vinay before he left and said, 'Please come after my exam. I couldn't talk with you Properly due to preparation.'

Vinay replied, 'I will definitely come again.'

But Lalita thought, 'He will never come because I have disturbed him in the night.'

She said to Vinay, 'Please forgive me. I disturbed you last night.'

Vinay said, 'Don't worry. I know very well that love is blind. I am same like you, dying to meet my sweetheart. But I have respect for your love. Please forgive me.'

Lalita said, 'When will you meet me next time?'

'I don't know. Whenever God likes us to meet.'

Vinay read Lalita's sad face and said, 'What is this? You cannot control your life like this. Control yourself and believe in God. You will feel better. Please forget me, otherwise you will be in great trouble.'

'I am already in trouble.'

'I have already told you in very clear words that I love Jaya Khan only. I can't even think about others and you are still thinking about me. You have to forget everything otherwise your life will be in trouble. I can help you every step but not on this matter.'

Lalita replied, 'How can I forget those college days and our meeting and all?

'Vinay said as much as possible you have to forget this.'

She listened to Vinay and sank into a sea of sadness. She dropped him and came back to her house. Vinay went to his home too.

Lalita become very sad after Vinay left. She thought about the room of Vinay, where she had stayed three times. 'But now I cannot go there because he has left that room and he will never go there.' She came to her room and slept on her bed. Pearl of tears dropped from her beautiful eyes.her heart was saying my love destiny is going to become stranger. Whom i love heartly he love someone else. God what i have done wrong with someone so i deserve this disunion in love

On the other hand, Vinay reached his home. Payal came fast and saw that her uncle had a bag.

Vinay understood Payal's feeling and that she wanted something from him. Then he remembered, 'I forgot even jalebi for Payal due to Lalita.'

Then he took out an apple from the bag and gave it to her. As Payal was an eight-year-old, so she gave the apple to her grandma.

Vinay touched his mother's feet and sat on the chair with his mother. As they conversed, his mother asked him, 'Where is your smile? You are not looking well.'

'Mother, I was very busy, so I am looking like that.'

'You are right. Work by heart but you don't have to take tension. Your work will be complete. You worry about you, loss of your weight even, my son.' She was talking and patting his head too. So he forgot everything because of which he had tension.

Vinay said, 'Whenever I come to you, all my tension is over.'

His mother laughed at Vinay; she said, 'Then why do you live away from me, my son?' They continued talking. After this, he met all in the evening; after having food, Vinay slept because he hadn't been able to sleep properly for the last two nights.

# 18

## Vinay Meets Jaya and Rukhsar, Album Complete

The next day, Vinay went to Jaya's home to see he
He wanted to explain everything to her.

Then he reached her home and said, 'That day you
went away without seeing me. Why are you angry with
me after all?'

She said, 'Your fiancée had come here. She was
talking about you that you are not a good man, You are
playboy.'

Vinay understood that all this Tara's father had
explained (about Lalita and him) to Tara and Tara told
Jaya.

Vinay cleared this point; in the meanwhile, Rukhsar
came. She said to Vinay, 'You have come here after a
long time.'

Vinay said, 'You are right. I was busy in my job at
the studio.'

She said, 'I know you were so busy. But what is my
sister's fault? Why is she getting punishment of waiting
for you?'

Vinay became nervous; he thought that Jaya had told the entire story about Lalita and him to Rukhsar. He apologised and said, 'I am not guilty.'

'There is no need to apologise, but you have to understand her feelings. She is waiting for you since a long time. You should have respect for her love.'

Then he realised that she was talking about another topic. Vinay said, 'Whatever I am doing, it is only to get her love. I want to see her always happy. You think I don't love Jaya. I love Jaya as much as she loves me. I always think about her when I do my job in the studio also.'

After listening to this, Jaya felt that maybe Vinay was right.

While Vinay and Rukhsar were talking, Vinay's boss's call came on his phone. He said, 'Come immediately. Your album is going to be released.'

On hearing this, Vinay's face became sad because he couldn't speak to Jaya about that misunderstanding about Lalita and him; he couldn't explain to Jaya that he was right.

Vinay said, 'Jaya, wait for me. I will come back soon.'

Rukhsar laughed at his sentence and said, 'She is doing the same waiting for you.'

Vinay came back to his home immediately. He touched his parents' feet, giving respect, and left for the studio.

On the other hand, Jaya had doubts about Vinay. She thought, 'Maybe the call was from that girl who was with Vinay at the temple near the old well, Tara was right but I am sure Vinay cannot be a playboy.'

He reached the music studio. As soon as he reached there, everybody started clapping. Many people were waiting to see Vinay. Then he reached the stage.

His boss said, 'Vinay, today your hard work is a success now.'

A cameraman asked Vinay, 'Now that this album "*Lover of Previous Birth*" is going to released, would you like to say something to our viewers?'

Then Vinay said, 'To all, I want to say only this that this album is a special part of my life. This is the clue to my love story. I have sung these for her. I mean, I have written these songs in her love. If she is watching me on television, then I want to say something to her. I love you very much. I know you are very angry with me. Please forgive me.

'Along with this, I want to say something more. If you want a successfull life, first, you need to decide a destiny in life. Without destiny this life is useless. To reach your destiny, first, you have to change your way of thinking what I mean is that you have to stop making excuses, to not be afraid of failing, to eliminate negativity and procrastination. Such kind of thinking interrupt you. But don't be afraid of problems also. Compete with life. Your destiny is waiting for you Don't depand on fate, work hard with determination. I am sure you will write your own fate. For this, you only need courage and confidence which reside in every one. We only we have to develop this confidence. Always think positive then everything will be positive. Keep in mind that destiny is dependent on good thought and not in making excuses or being lazy.

My life is so good because of the contribution of my parents. I wouldn't be a success without my father's support. Even this life is not complete without him. My mother is greater than God. And this life is given by her. I haven't seen my own mother, but it is true that I didn't realise that I am not her own son. Today whatever I am is a blessing of her. Whenever I was not well, she read my face and asked me why I was sad and solved my problem. I mean, I don't have to explain to her my problem. My mother automatically knows my problem. She is an affectionate mother. The smell of her affection will never be found in flowers or any scent. In her feet is my heaven. We all realise it when we are away from our mother. Finally, I want to say that don't stay away from me, my mother, otherwise I won't live.'

Everybody clapped. All eyes became tearful. Because of this interview, the sale of the album was very good. Everybody liked Vinay's song. After this album, his name came in the list of singers. He got many offers from different companies. But he didn't accept any at that time.

People were impressed by this interview. Now Jaya too thought that Vinay's love was only for her. It was a misunderstanding between them.

Her eyes became tearful because of happiness. She realised that Vinay had done this only for their happiness. He lived away from her so that he could do something for their life.

On the other hand, his mother felt proud of her son that her son was one among a million. He loved her much more than her own son.

He became famous with this album; his director gave to him a cheque of ten million rupees.

Now Vinay's name was changed to Vinay Shrivastav. Vinay's fiancée, Tara, was happy to know that Vinay had become a singer. But in this happiness there was a little sadness also. She thought that Vinay had gone away from her in this love race. She was quite disturbed to think about when would Vinay come. 'My love is only for Vinay, but he is not mine now.'

Vinay reached his house and touched his father's feet. He gave the ten-million-rupee cheque which he had got from the director; he said, 'This is my small gift for you. You have done a lot of obligation in my life how will I pay this debt? Please take this money.'

His mother said, 'What are you doing? You are showing us money. This is not good. Today you have made us realise that we are your stepparents only.'

'Mother, I want to offer my success and hard work to you.'

His father said, 'You have already made our name famous. This is enough, my son. God bless you, my son.'

'Father, I don't need so much happiness that I forget my parents.' His brother Raja congratulated him too. He got many phone calls due to this success.

After meeting all, he said to his mother, 'I am going to meet Jaya. That day, the boss had called me, so I could not explain to her about the misunderstanding.'

'OK, my son, go, my son, but come in time.'

Then Vinay reached Jaya. He said, 'Jaya, your Mohit has come to you.' She hugged him. Seeing her facial expression, he felt that she had forgiven him.

He thought that he had got all the happiness of the world.

Vinay said, 'The time of our wedding is coming near now.'

She said, 'Yes, Vinay, we have waited for this a long time.'

They were talking when Rukhsar came and said, 'You are taking away my sister from me. I will be lonely. You are taking her with you to your home.'

'No, Rukhsar, how can I take her to my home now? It is possible only after our wedding.'

Rukhsar laughed at Vinay's reply. Rukhsar said, 'You have scared me by saying that you are taking away my sister from me now.'

Jaya said, 'Vinay, I have waited for you for a long time. Now don't keep me away from your life for a lifetime otherwise I won't live.

Vinay said, 'I will stay always with you, my sweetheart. Let's go to the city today. I will show you the city.'

They all departed from there for city.

'You are taking my sister to the city for the first time.'

'Yes, Rukhsar, you are right,' Vinay said.

'So you are doing a job in the studio and you didn't tell us. Why?'

Vinay said, 'You are right I didn't tell you about my work. But it is my thinking If you are sure about your destiny, work so silently that after your success, people will know this without information. So there is no need to explain to everyone about realising your destiny before success. Once our work is complete people will know it automatically.'

After listening to Vinay's answer, Rukhsar felt that Vinay was a high-thinking man.

Jaya said, 'We will come back in time?'

Vinay said, 'Don't worry. We will come back in time.'

After some time, they reached the city. Vinay said at the shop, 'Buy a dress as you like.'. Jaya and Rukhsar bought dresses for themselves. And Jaya bought one dress for Vinay also.

Vinay liked the dress which Jaya bought for him. After shopping, they went to a hotel. Vinay ordered for food. He asked Jaya and Rukhsar, 'Anything else you want to buy?'

'Not now. We should go home otherwise we will be late.'

Rukhsar said, 'I want ice cream, Vinay.' Vinay brought ice cream for Jaya and Rukhsar.

They went back home. Vinay said again, 'After some days, we will be one (wed).'

Rukhsar thought, 'Now Jaya is going away from me. With whom will I live? My mother is not there with me. My father is not there with me. And now my sister is going away from me too.' Her heart was beating fast, thinking about this. 'Who will help me?' Her face became sad.

Seeing this, Jaya became sad too. She said to Rukhsar, 'Don't worry. Believe in Allah.' Jaya wiped the tears flowing from Rukhsar's eyes. She said, 'You always be happy. I will send you money. After my wedding, stay at our aunt's house (their mother's sister). We will be in touch by phone, Rukhsar, and everything will be fine. Keep believing in God.'

'But, Didi (sister), how will I live without you? Since childhood both of us have lived with each other. And after some days, you will go away from me forever.'

'Rukhsar, I am not going away from you. Whenever you think about me or feel lonely, you pray to Allah. He will definitely listen to your prayers.'

# 19

# Marriage of Jaya and Vinay

Vinay came back to his home after dropping Jaya and Rukhsar. He explained to his mother, 'I am going to marry Jaya.'

His mother said, 'Are you going to marry Jaya? I will see a girl for you. Do not marry her.'

His face became sad.

'You are a singer now, you will get a good girl for wedding.'

'No, Mom, I like her very much and she also likes me the same. I won't marry anyone other than her.'

'How much more she likes you than me?'

'No, Mom, you are great. Nobody loves more than you.'

Then he explained his love story to his mother, 'I was hiding something from you. Now the time has come to explain this to you. She has remembered all about our previous birth. She says that we were lovers from a previous birth and we had played in this temple.'

His mother said, 'She is definitely telling a lie. She loves your wealth, not you. She is making a story to get your name. And you are going to be mad for her?

You don't know girls can cheat for wealth and name nowadays.'

'Yes, Mother, you are right, but you know she loved me when I was nothing. And I used to say to you also that I get a dream of a girl and a song which I had sung in college I have heard that song for the first time from her. Whenever I go to that temple, I feel that I have come there many times and I'm reminded of the previous birth too.'

Vinay's mother realised that Vinay was right.

She said, 'OK, Vinay, as you wish.'

Then his father came. He said, 'Vinay, I also agree with you, but you don't know. We had fixed your engagement with Tara. In childhood, Tara and you were best friends. And you knew her very well. Now if I will break off this relationship, then her father will become angry. He expects that this relation is still the same like before.'

Then Vinay said, 'Can you break it off?'

'How can I break it up, my son? This is fixed by our relatives. Break-off is not so easy as you are thinking. When you were small, a local court had called on some problem of the village. That time, this relationship was fixed by us. This matter is so old I know, but it is still the same like before. He is my friend and our relationship is good otherwise he can call a local court any time again if we break off this relationship.'

Vinay thought, 'I have to marry Tara so that this relationship will remain the same. And I can do my duty for my parents. They had brought me up. They had made my life so easy, and today I am becoming selfish. I am a very bad man. For my happiness, I am destroying the happiness of my parents. This is not fair. How can I do this sin? But I have promised to my sweetheart Jaya Khan also. So how can I manage it? This time only God can save me from this problem.'

He said to his father, 'I am ready to marry.'

Then his father made a call to Tara's father, 'We are ready for marriage. I and my son have also agreed. Please come here.'

On hearing this, Tara became so happy. 'Today I won my love.' Her father came to Vinay's home.

Tara's father asked Vinay, 'Please give it another thought. Don't take any wrong decision in a hurry. Otherwise both your lives will be destroyed, and we also will not live happy. Think and tell us.'

'I respect your great idea, but I can't see my parents unhappy,' he was saying when his mother came and said, 'Don't destroy your life because of us. If you want to marry Jaya Khan, then I will support you. But don't take a wrong decision.'

Vinay did not reply. He was silent. They knew what Vinay wanted.

# 20

## Painful Moment for Tara When Vinay Gets Married

After that, Tara's father went back to his home. After coming to know that Vinay had chosen his bride Tara lost her head. She became sad and went to her room. She closed the door from inside. She recalled all the memories she had of Vinay. Tears dropped from her eyes. She wanted to sleep and drift into her memories of Vinay, but she could not sleep.

She thought, 'We played games together in childhood. But in those games there was a game which belonged to my personal life. He made me wife, but it was only a game. Why did I think it was realty? Dream is always a dream. It never becomes reality. But in my dream, my prince had come, and my waiting was over for him. And I was feeling that he will come and take me with him forever. But now I have woken up. And my dream is ended. In the race between Jaya Khan and me, she won the love of Vinay and I am the loser. Now my Vinay has gone quite far away from me. In this race of love, he is so far away from me that I cannot even see him. And I will not see him forever. He has left me behind. By God's grace, he will never have any problem. I didn't get my destiny but he may get his destiny.'

Her father knocked on the door again and again, but she didn't open. He said, 'My daughter, please open the door and have food.'

She replied, 'I am not hungry. Don't wait for me and you have food.'

'But at least open the door. I am worried about you.' Her father knew this that whenever she became angry she would do like this.

After a long time, she opened the door. He felt bad to see her sad face.

Her father said, 'Don't worry, my daughter. Believe in God. God will definitely listen to your wish.' After listening to her father, She felt better than before.

On that side, preparations for marriage of Vinay started. All arrangements were started with fanfare. Vinay was dressed like a groom. That side, Jaya was dressed like a bride as per Muslim tradition. Her disunion was now going to be over. She was very happy.

Vinay and Jaya both were happy from inside. They were going to get their lover. Vinay called Tara and Lalita for his marriage.

Tara was somewhat happy that Vinay would get his lover because she wants to see Vinay happy. But Lalita considered Jaya an enemy. After the party, people went back to their homes. And Lalita came back to her home too. But she could not compose herself. Her heart was weeping for Vinay. She made a call to Vinay. She said to

Vinay, 'Come immediately to Pintu Park. I am waiting for you here.'

'Right now I am not allowed to go out of home.'

Lalita said, 'You must come. I have to say something to you.'

'Lalita, what is the matter after all? Please tell me on the phone.'

She said, 'It is not possible to tell on the phone. It is very urgent, so come fast.'

It was the golden night of Vinay, but Lalita was calling him. He was thinking, 'What should I do?'

Then he went to Jaya and said, 'Lalita is calling me right now.'

'Vinay, you can go, but tell her that Jaya Khan wants to meet you.'

Vinay reached the place she had called him. He said, 'Lalita, what is the matter? I did not even meet my wife and you called me here.'

'Vinay, you are saying you don't know what the matter is, what is going on with me, and how I am. That night you passed with me, and now you have married Jaya Khan. And you know that day at the bus stop we had embraced each other and it was live recording and everyone watching, so people had seen us in such a state.'

Vinay said, 'You had done a mistake. You hugged me.'

'OK, forget whatever happened that day, but now who will marry me?'

'Yes, Lalita, I understand what is going on with you. But the mistake was done by you, and it is the job of media to find such a scene.'

'But, Vinay, I am in love with you. Tell me what I should do. I will not live without you.'

'Lalita, you have to search a good handsome boy and marry him. For that, even I can help to find a boy for you.'

She said, 'I am not joking. I can't live without you.'

'You know that I love Jaya. I can't share my love with another. I like only Jaya, all right. She is waiting for me since a long time. I have saved my love only for her. I had told you that we are lovers from birth after birth. And you don't understand this.'

She said, 'I don't feel good without you.'

Vinay said, 'I want to live my life in a good way. I accept that you had given bail for me without being an acquaintance. But now you want to defame me.'

'Vinay, you are wrong. You have defamed me, not I. Vinay, if I want I can go to court, but I love you, so I don't want to see you in trouble.'

'Now I am getting late. I am going. Jaya is waiting for me.'

Lalita said, 'Don't go after leaving me. I am trustee of your love, Vinay. I can't live without you. Whatever you like, I will do. But don't go without me. I will die without you.'

'You have gone mad, Lalita. You are very beautiful. I know your heart is pure. You will definitely get a good boy for marriage. I had explained to you to not wait for me. You will be in trouble.'

Then he was gone from there. Except tears, nothing else was in her eyes. She liked Vinay and Vinay liked someone else. Because of this, she got depressed.

He came back to his home. He was very happy for Jaya. Today was the golden night of their marriage. There were no guests at home. His heart was beating fast. He was waiting for her since a long time. Then he went to Jaya. But that time Payal was talking with Jaya. She said, 'Uncle, finally you got married with this angel.'

'You were right, but she was Rukhsar that day in college.'

Payal said, 'Both are same and beautiful. But from now you are my aunt.'

Payal and Jaya were talking when Payal's mother came and said, 'Come, Payal, it is sleep time.'

'Mom, I will sleep with my aunt.'

Payal's mother said, 'Your father brought a game for you.' Payal became excited on hearing about the game. She ran fast to her father.

She said to her father, 'Where is my game?'

Her father said, 'Take, this is your game.'

She was happy to see such a nice game. She said, 'I am going to show this game to my Jaya aunt.'

Her mother said, 'She has gone to sleep. Show to her tomorrow. This is your sleep time.'

So she slept.

Vinay went to Jaya and said, 'Lalita made me crazy, Jaya.'

'What happened?'

Vinay told Jaya everything about Lalita and his relationship. 'She is my best friend since college. Once upon a time, she bailed me when I had to go to jail. She likes me very much. I have told her everything about our love, but she can't understand.'

She said, 'Vinay, forget it. Start another topic.'

Vinay said, 'OK, so how do you find it here?'

'I am finding it good here.'

'You are looking very charming. In this dress, you are looking like a princess. I am so lucky to get a wife like you.'

I am too lucky to get you in this birth. But in our family life of women is hell. People don't send girl to school. Girl cannot choose boy for marry. Girls are under boundation of family.their life like jail bird.

Vinay said this is not good, people should change their thinking. Respect to women feeling and girl should choose her life patner herself.

'But i made you wait for long time please forgive me even i have not respect your feeling you are very good girl Jaya khan

Jaya said, 'Don't appreciate me otherwise your friend Lalita will feel bad.'

Jaya what can I do for her I am helpless.

'Forget it. Let's enjoy our meeting.' Then they both embraced each other and went to sleep.

A week after their wedding, he got many offers for singing in big companies. He was thinking, 'I now I have to shift to Mumbai, and I will take Jaya and my mom with me.'

# 21

## Vinay Goes to Mumbai and Archit Meets Lalita

Vinay and Jaya got ready to go Mumbai. He thought, 'Before I move, I have to do something for Lalita.' His friend Archit came in Vinay's mind; in college days, Archit loved Lalita very much. 'Because of me he couldn't develop his friendship with Lalita

Vinay called Archit at home. He said to Archit, 'How are you, Archit?'

'I am fine, Vinay,' Archit replied.

Vinay said, 'You know Lalita loves me very much. She is love mad after me. She can't live without me. But I love Jaya Khan. I don't want that she destroys her life. And I know this, you love Lalita very much. You didn't talk in college time because I was her close friend. I know her. She is a very pure-hearted girl, I mean very honest. If you don't mind, do me a favour. You propose to her and say to her your inside feeling. I know you like her very much since college days.'

Archit said, 'What are you talking about, Vinay? It isn't possible. And how can I do this? Even she has forgotten me. Even she doesn't know me properly.'

Vinay said, 'Will you not say to her what is in your heart? Even you like her very much. You are going to get your love and you are ignoring it. You will not get this opportunity in life. Say to her otherwise you will be late.'

Archit said, 'I cannot do this.'

Vinay said, 'I was expecting that you will do this favour for me, but you have destroyed all my hope.'

Archit said, 'I agree, but from where do I have to start?'

Then Vinay explained, 'You first call her at Pintu Park. Say to her, "I want to tell you something. I was afraid that you will insult me, so I didn't speak to you. Don't deny me. If you don't like me, you can go in silence. But don't refuse me otherwise my heart will feel very bad." You also say to her, "I wanted to say this from college days, but you were busy with someone else."'

Archit said, 'I am afraid that she will slap me.'

'Don't worry. She is not such a kind of girl. This is the list of her favourite items.'

After he explained this lesson to Archit he went to Bombay.

After Vinay and Jaya's wedding, Rukhsar became lonely. She was feeling very bad without her sister Jaya Khan. Rukhsar thought, 'My sister had told me that whenever you feel lonely you remember Allah. Everything will be ordinary.' So she did same. After a few days, Rukhsar went to her aunt's home (her mother's sister). But her aunt was very angry with Jaya's wedding. Her aunt said, 'At least, she should have chosen a boy from our religion instead of that other cast boy. I had explained to your father this. Do the wedding of both daughters, but he did not accept my advice. And now we have to see this day. People are talking about this wedding.'in our cast women is under boundation, we don't have to cross our limit. We are like jail bird. Only elder choose boy and girl for marry Keep in mind you too.

Rukhsar felt like her aunt was scoffing her. 'My aunt is not happy to see me here.' She said to her aunt, 'Please stop for God's sake.'

When she heard this, she became angrier. 'I am saying to you about reality and you are silencing me. You want to do like Jaya. She has destroyed our family name.'

After listening to this, Rukhsar became upset. She thought, 'I made a mistake in coming here.' And she started to weep.

Then her aunt realised, 'Why I am scoffing her? It's useless. There is no fault of hers. This misdeed was done by Jaya. Today if her mother, my sister, was alive in this world, then she would never forgive me.'

Her aunt felt that she was same as her daughter and she was making her weep. 'Please forgive me, Rukhsar. Due to me you are weeping. Allah will never forgive.' Then she embraced her. After this, their relationship became like before.

There Vinay was thinking, 'After getting Archit's friendship, Lalita will forget me and her life will be a pleasure. They are my college friends.'

Vinay got an offer from a company, then he shifted into the company flat (house). He started his singing job again in a new company. He sang a song:

*I am mad keen in your love.*
*I am dying in your flirtation.*
*Life of love, live with me.*
*Now we are for your mad keen.*
*I am mad keen in your love!*
*This love is hankering after you*
*My heart is beating fast only for you*
*I won't leave without your love.*
*Don't deny in life for something*
*In my dwell your swear.*
*I am mad keen in your love!*

*Since when I met you there.*
*Came out flower of love there*
*Magic of your love played on me*
*I enjoy our meeting in the dream everytime*
*Now we become one for birth and birth*
*I am mad keen in your love.*

After listening to this song, his boss said, 'Really, you have talent. We take time to make a song once a month and you have done this only in four days. How you have done this?'

Vinay said, 'Sir, I start my work heartily (full effort). Along with it, I give target to my team that you have to do this today. And they do their job with inside in given time. If you do any work with inside, then everything is possible.'

As he listened to Vinay, his boss thought, 'Vinay is not only artist but also he is an intelligent, hard-working person.'

He sang a new song and he got a new reward for their effort. Gradually, his name reached the sky.

# 22

# Sadness of Tara

This side there the fiancée of Vinay, Tara, declined to marry. Her father was quite disturbed due to this. She said, 'I won't marry. You have forgotten my childhood promise.'

Her father said, 'Yes, I remembered that promise, but no can do anything against fate. Please forget everything and believe in God. Everything will be well and good.' Then her father narrated to her a tale. 'An old woman always worried about her son. She every day prayed to almighty and said," give my son a good job. And help me to get him married" One day she had a dream of almighty. And almighty said to her, "You worry about your son only, but I have worry about the entire world. Do meditation. Keep attention on me, sit in thoughtless state and forget all problems and leave it on me. All your problems will be solved automatically."

'After listening to almighty, she did the same as said by almighty. She forgot all her problems. And she put all her attention on almighty. Then she felt the power of almighty.

Why we worry about problem of our and other. All work is done by almighty. From our breath to animals, trees, birds, all live their life as per God's rule and they all are happy. This all is running by God's power. There is no means of our worry, then why do we worry about them? If we think about all problems and worry, then God will think that they are already busy in their own problems. They do not turst me.

As per God, the old woman had done the same. She kept her attention on God. Within a week, her son got a job and the next week his engagement was fixed.'

After listening to this story narrated by her father, she reduced her burden of worry. Her father said, 'I have left all tension and problems on God. Now God will do everything well.'

On the other side, Archit called Lalita to Pintu Park. It was the same place where Vinay and Lalita had met. At first, Lalita refused to come to Pintu Park. After Archit requested to Lalita, then she agreed to come.

Lalita said to Archit angrily, 'What is matter after all? Why have you called me here?'

Then Archit said, 'I love you very much since a long time. I feared that you will insult me because you are very beautiful and I am not fit for you.

'I feared that you will refuse my proposal and you will insult me in front of everyone. So I could not say my heart's voice. I have been keenly in love since that time.

'You don't know how much I love you. No one can have loved anyone like me. I was worried about you that you were like someone else. But you are a very good girl and beautiful too.

Hearing this, Lalita said, 'Don't make a story before me. That day I had refused and I had told you that I like someone else.'

Then Archit said, 'Still you love him?'

She replied, what do you mean by still you love him, of course I love him so much.'

Archit asked, 'How much does he love you?'

Then Lalita could not give an answer to Archit; she was speechless.

Archit said, 'Then why are you love mad after him? You should forget him.'

Lalita said, how can i forget him he is in my heart

He is love some else then why do you think about him. Said Archit

Lalita relizes Archit is right, she said 'There is one thing more. You don't know about my previous life. You will know it, then you will go away from me.' Archit said, 'I don't want to listen to what is your previous life. I am only love mad after you. And since I have seen you, I have had a dream that I want to live in your arms.

'If you will refuse today, I will be burn in you disunion, but I won't marry someone else for life time. This is my final decision. You have to only believe in me.'

Then Lalita thought, 'Whom I loved, he didn't care for my love. And this Archit who loves me, there is no limit to his love.' She said to Archit, 'I will accept your love. Not now. I will tell you after some days. Let me go now.'

The next day Archit called her to the same place. He gifted a watch to her.

After seeing the watch, she said, 'How do you know I like this watch?' She was happy and kissed his hand.

Then Archit said, 'I have loved you. I have found out since last two years about what you like and what you don't like. I know this too what you eat in the morning and what you like to eat before you go to sleep. Blue jeans and yellow T-shirt you like very much. You like to jog in the evening. And you don't like tea.'

Then Lalita said, 'Really, you like me very much. Today I found out that someone loves me so much.'

'Yes, Lalita, you are right. I love you very much. There is no limit to my love. You know it now, but I knew this since the day I loved you that one day you will be my lover.'

Lalita embraced Archit. Archit thanked Vinay from inside because it was due to Vinay he got his first love.

Lalita said, 'What are you thinking?'

'I am thinking about you, Lalita' said Archit.

Lalita said, 'Don't deceive me otherwise I won't live. I was already hurt by someone. I cannot tolerate some more heart aches. Please take what i am saying seriously.'

Gradually, she started liking Archit very much.

And both became lovers.

One day, Archit made a call to Vinay But he was busy so he couldn't pick up Archit call. In the evening, Archit went to meet Lalita. They both went to the hotel where Vinay and Lalita had eaten food. Then Lalita thought about Vinay.

Then Archit said, 'What are you thinking?'

'I cannot tell you, Vinay,' she said.

'What you cannot say to me? Still you think of me as a stranger?'

'Archit, I am thinking about him whom I had loved. But I love you. Thinking about him is useless.'

After having food, he dropped Lalita at her home.

Archit came back to his home and made a call to Vinay. This time Vinay was available and he picked up his call. Archit thanked Vinay and said, 'I got my love due to your help. She has accepted my love. Now if she will know that this has done by you, then she would feel very bad.'

Vinay said, 'She is a very good girl. If you will marry her, your life will be set. You cannot get a girl like her in life. Take this seriously.'

Archit said, 'You are right, Vinay. She is a very good-natured girl. Her attitude is very attractive. Her heart is pure. But if she will not agree to marry then?'

Vinay said, 'She will agree, but you keep in mind never to deceive her. Whatever I am saying, please note it. OK, bye-bye.'

In the evening time, Archit called Lalita and said to her, 'I love you, Lalita. I can't wait anymore. I want to marry you. Please don't refuse my proposal otherwise my heart will break.'

Then she gave the green signal. And in a few days, they were married. They carried on with their lives. Their good time was to start.

After some days, Vinay made a call to Archit. First, he congratulated Archit then asked, 'How was your wedding?' But this time, Lalita heard the conversation when she picked up another phone extension in the home. Then Lalita understood the entire plan of Vinay. After the conversation, Vinay disconnected the call. But Lalita was shocked that she had been again deceived by someone. Her eyes became tearful.

But that time, she didn't speak to Archit about this matter. In the evening Archit said, 'Come, Lalita, for dinner.' She came, but she couldn't eat food properly because of Vinay and Archit's plan.

Archit asked her, 'What happened? Why aren't you eating food like usual?' She didn't reply to Archit and went to bed. Archit came to her and asked her, 'What is the matter after all, Lalita? What is the problem? Why are you not talking to me and why are you so sad?'

Lalita didn't reply to Archit and started weeping.

Then Archit said, 'You swear to me. You have to tell me what is the matter otherwise how will I solve your problem.'

Then she said, 'You had cheated with me. Have I done wrong with you that you are taking revenge on me?'

Archit understood what she wanted to say. He replied to Lalita, 'Yes, this entire plan was by Vinay, but this is the truth. I love you very much. If it is not the truth, then why did I marry you? Please believe me. I love you very much. If my wedding had not taken place with you, I would not have got a better girl than you. I am really happy with you.'

Then she felt some relief. She said to Archit, 'Don't deceive me in life otherwise your Lalita won't live.' Hearing this, Archit hugged Lalita.

Then their love became like it had been the previous day.

# 23

# Love of Rukhsar and Salim

That side, Rukhsar, sister of Jaya Khan, lived with her aunt (her mother's sister). Now the relationship between her aunt and Rukhsar had become good. But she was thinking, 'Why am I a burden on my aunt? I have to do a job.' This idea came in Rukhsar's mind because of her female friends.

She said to her aunt, 'I want to do a job.'

Her aunt said, 'You don't need to do a job. If you need something, ask me.'

But she didn't obey her aunt. She made a plan to go look for a job after consulting with other village girls. The next day, Rukhsar got ready for her job.

Rukhsar's aunt said, 'If your parents had been alive, then you wouldn't have to do a job. All this is because of me. I am not giving you all facilities, so you are going to earn money.'

Rukhsar said to her aunt, 'For how many days will I depend on you? I have to live this life and I have to set up my home. If I do not see outside life, then I will have to depend on someone else and listen to the taunts of people. I want to learn how to live this life full of struggle. We were born poor. This is our fate, but if we die poor, then this is an unsuccessful life.'

Her aunt thought, 'Yes, you are right, my daughter.'

So she started a job. One day, a boy whose name was Salim saw Rukhsar and said, 'Yaa Allah, what a beautiful girl! But why is she doing such hard work? It is not right to do a job, such hard work for such a beautiful girl.' He wanted to talk with her, but he was afraid that she would throw abuses at him. So he didn't talk with her. He only saw her from a distance.

Rukhsar found out that someone wanted to talk with her. But she came home quietly. She said to her aunt, 'I have learnt many tasks today. And today I felt very good at my job.'

Her aunt said, 'This is very good, Rukhsar. You have the attitude of learning. This will give you a successful life.'

Then Rukhsar thought, 'I have to call my sister, Jaya.' Then she made a call to Jaya and said, 'Didi (sister), I went for a job today.'

Jaya felt very bad after listening to Rukhsar. She said, 'Please forgive me, Rukhsar. I haven't sent you a money order, so you have done this all. From today, I will send money order on time.'

Rukhsar said, 'No problem you haven't sent me money order. This is good for my life. I will get the opportunity to see the outside life and learn how to earn.'

Jaya said, 'Don't go again, for job. This is my duty to send you money.

'OK, Didi (sister), I will not go again.'

Then they talked with each other.

On the other hand, Salim became love mad in love after Rukhsar. He made plans to talk with Rukhsar. The next day in the company, Rukhsar was coming from one side and Salim was going to the other side. Salim knew that Rukhsar was coming; he turned his eyes to the other side and bumped into Rukhsar. He said, 'I am sorry. Are you OK?'

Rukhsar said, 'I am OK.' She started to go away from there, but her bag had dropped on the floor.

Salim said, 'Stop, beautiful girl, take this. It dropped because of me.'

She smiled and said, 'Thanks.'

'There is no need to say thank you. This is my duty, but I want to say something to you.'

Rukhsar said, 'OK, say what you want to say to me.'

He said, 'Not now. This is not a good time to say about my feelings.'

Rukhsar said, 'OK, whenever you feel that this is a good time tell me what you want.'

Salim thought, 'If it will be late, this will be a problem for me.' He said to Rukhsar, 'I want to meet you alone.'

Rukhsar said, 'Why should I meet you?' Even she knew that he was the one who saw her silently and she knew that he liked her.

Then Salim said to Rukhsar, 'I like you.'

On listening to this Rukhsar said, 'How can this be possible?'

Then Salim said, 'I want to marry you. I will take care of you in life. You stay at home. I will earn.'

Rukhsar said, 'Stop it. It is enough.' And she came back to her duty without replying to him. After her duty got over, she went back to her aunt's home.

She said to her aunt, 'Today Salim has asked me about marriage.'

Her aunt said, 'This is good for you. All my tension will be over if this will be done.' Then her aunt went to Salim's house and talked to Salim's uncle and aunt about Salim and Rukhsar's marriage.

Salim's uncle said to Rukhsar's aunt, 'You don't know. He has no wealth, even if you would like to do marriage of Rukhsar and Salim.'

'There is no need for wealth. They like each other. I think they will start to earn for their love.'

Salim's uncle said, 'We don't have any problem. We do not interfere in his life.'

'I am saying this to you because his parents are not around anymore. So you are equal to his parents. And we came to know if you have any problem about this marriage. So that we will not face any problem in future.'

Then Salim's uncle said, 'It is good. We agree to this relationship.'

Then Rukhsar aunts came back home and said to Rukhsar, 'Salim's father is no more. But I have talked with his uncle. They are agreeing to this relationship.'

After listening to this, Rukhsar said, 'You too want to go away from me.'

'No, my daughter. I would you to stay always here, but this is a law of society that we all have to get our life partner. This is the social order also.' Then they talked among themselves.

# 24

# Vinay Comes Home and Meets His Friends

On that side, Vinay had not gone to his village for a long time. So he took a leave for some days and went back to his hometown. He was very happy to meet his family and parents.

His mother said, 'Have you forgotten us? After a long time, you didn't even remember us?'

Then Vinay said, 'I always think about you. But I don't have time to come here.'

Jaya said, 'We had tried to come, but Vinay's album is not finished.'

Then Payal said, 'Uncle, why are you coming here after a long time? I am every day thinking about you and that when will my uncle come.'

Then Vinay tried to make Payal understand, 'I was busy.' She came and sat on the lap of Vinay. Then they talked to each other. Vinay gave her jalebi.

Payal said, 'You still remember my sweet dish?'

Vinay said, 'How can I forget it?'

Then Vinay's brother and sister-in-law came. They were glad to meet Vinay. Raja was happy to know of Vinay success. Now his brother saw him with respectful eyes.

Raja Bhaiya hugged Vinay and said, 'Did you forgive me?'

Vinay laughed at Raja's sentence. Vinay said to Raja Bhaiya, 'You still remember that incident? This is not good, Brother.' Then they all laughed.

Then Vinay's sister-in-law said, 'Your brother has totally changed, like you.'

'Yes, these are Vinay's morals.'

After that, Vinay met everyone. The next day, they went to that old temple. They sat there for some time and talked.

Vinay said, 'We had met here for the first time, do you know this.'

'I know this. I was waiting for you here. I had done mediation here. Due to that, I got you.'

Vinay said, 'I like this temple very much, and this came in my dreams many times.' His memory became refreshed. He said, 'This is the place where our love started.'

'Yes, Vinay, you are right. Our love started from here in our previous life.'

Vinay said, 'Please tell me what happened to us. Why did people kill me and throw in that well?'

Jaya said, 'That story is very long. I will tell you at an appropriate time.'

'You have already told me you will tell this at an appropriate time. When will this time come?'

'Vinay, I cannot say about the future. Stop talking on this topic.'

Vinay said, 'When I come here, I feel peace here.'

'Yes, Vinay, I too feel peaceful here.'

Then Vinay realised that in this temple, the existence of god's love is there (god stay there). He said, 'We have to repair this temple.'

After some time, they went back home.

Jaya thought about her sister, 'I have to meet her.' But she remembered that Rukhsar was at her aunt's home and her aunt was unhappy with Vinay's and her wedding, so she changed her plan to meet her.

Vinay said to Jaya, 'I am going to meet my friends.' He left home. Vinay made a call to Jai and Archit and said, 'Come to the park of the college. I am waiting for you here. Just come here.'

While Vinay waited for Jai and Archit to come there, he saw his college and was reminded of his previous days; he moved around the entire campus. First he went to the main hall, where programmes and annual functions were often organised. Vinay thought, 'My class boys performed many times here, and I too performed here.' Then he saw the roof and thought, 'I have climbed on the roof many times with my friend.' He looked into the classroom through the window and thought about his student life. And he remembered his seat where he used to sit. He felt joy for his college and thought, 'I want to come again to this college. Again, I will enjoy with my friends. Again, I will play in this ground. What those days were of classes of English and maths!' After some time, he came and sat under a tree, where he had often attended classes many times. He was reminded of his old days.

He sang a song:

(student life has passed and now we are under responsibilities)
*Where has gone that day where has gone matters*
*Where has gone that friends and that interview*
*I remember that laughing tale of that day*
*Oh my God I want to be student again*
*Heart beating fast dampens my breath*
*Where has gone that day where has gone matters!*
*Without friend this life is not complete*
*Time has passed that all night*
*How can I forget that interview?*
*Where has gone that day where has gone matters!*
*Dwell in my heart all antics of my friends*
*Heart beating fast dampens my breath*
*Trust my eyes and my feeling of heart*
*Where has gone that day where has gone matters!*
*We had given excuse for coming late in class.*
*We went to bath in river after bunking class.*
*Without that memory nothing is life.*
*Where has gone that day where has gone matters!*
*How will come back those fine days*
*What is love of friend nobody knows it.*
*How can we live without friends?*
*Where has gone that day where has gone matters!*
*Where has gone that friends and that interview*
*I remember that laughing tale of that day*
*Oh my God I want to be student again*

*Heart beating fast dampens my breath*
*Where has gone that day where has gone matters!*

Then he got a call from Archit. 'My dear friend, where are you?'

Then Vinay said, 'I am lying on the grass in the ground of our college.'

Then both Jai and Archit came fast and hugged Vinay. Archit brought out cokes and snacks.

Vinay said, 'My friend, you have understood my feeling.' The three laughed at this sentence.

Vinay said, 'I have been waiting for this moment. I wanted that we enjoy in college like our previous days. But it is not possible to go back. Those days in this life are incomplete without friends. We had enjoyed our college days. But today it is lost like a needle in the sea between our responsibilities and helplessness. So we should enjoy every moment of life because it's never going to come back.'

Jai said, 'Vinay, you are right. I had forgotten everything, but you have reminded me.'

Vinay said, 'Today I have organised a party at my home.'

Archit asked, 'What time do I have to come?'

Vinay said, 'At eight o'clock. Listen to this carefully. Classmates who are connected with you call all of them and tell them that I have come here.'

Archit said, 'OK, Vinay, we will inform our classmates.'

Vinay asked, 'How is Lalita?'

'She is fine. Right now she is at home.'

'Take care of her all the time. She is a very innocent girl.'

'OK, Vinay, through you I got my love. Thank you very much.'

Vinay said, 'Don't mention it. You are my friend.'

Jai said, 'You have helped me in college days many times. I haven't even returned some money. You have helped me many times. How will I pay this debt.

Vinay said, 'Don't worry. Forget it.' Vinay started a new topic. 'You know in college time we used to go to those hills. Let's go there.'

Jai said, 'Yes, why not? You will not be coming here every day. Wherever you want to go, tell me.'

Then they went to the hills which were ten kilometres away from the village. After reaching there, they sat there for some time.

Vinay said, 'Some days before, there was a lake towards the temple. Is its water still the same or less?'

Jai said, 'I don't know. Even I had come here with you. Let's go and get Shri Mahadev's blessings.' They reached the temple, and after taking Shri Mahadev's blessing, they went towards the lake. They saw the lake which was looking very beautiful.

Archit said, 'This lotus is looking very beautiful. That time lotus was not there.'

'Yes, dear, what a beautiful scene this is. Some ducks are catching fish in the water.'

Vinay said, 'Through you, I have got the opportunity to refresh my memory. Tell me one thing. How are our classmates and what are they doing?'

Jai said, 'Some are doing good jobs out of state. And some have started their own business.'

'This is very good that they have got their way of life.'

Jai said, 'But I regret to say that one of our friends is not in this world.'

Vinay said nervously, 'Who?'

'Vinay, Raju is not among us any more,' said Jai.

'Oh, Raju was a very good person. What happened to him?'

Then Jai explained to Vinay, 'Two years earlier, he got married. We too went to his wedding. And after a year, Raju got a daughter. After some days, he got a new job. The next day, he had to join the new job. That night he was coming from the city. It was ten o'clock. In the night, he was coming towards the village. There was a truck coming from the opposite side. Likely the truck crushed him. After nearly half an hour, we reached there. We saw that he was not in a conscious state. He was breathing fast. We called an ambulance. I held him on my lap immediately. We reached the city hospital in a hurry, but the doctor refused to accept this case. The doctor said, "As fast as possible, take him to the main hospital." Then we went to the main hospital. On the way, his breathing became slow. In ten minutes, he took his last breath. And at eleven o'clock, he said his last bye to everyone.'

'Vinay, this is true that he had taken his last breath in my lap.'

After listening to this painful story, Vinay felt very sad. 'God, don't let anything like this to happen to someone.' His eyes became tearful.

Then they went back home. Vinay said bye to his friends and went back.

On seeing Vinay, his mother said, 'Where had you gone, my son? This Payal was searching for you for a long time and we also could not find you for a long time.'

Vinay said, 'What happened, Payal? Tell me.'

Payal said, 'You had gone without informing me. I was searching for you because I thought you had gone to Mumbai without me. I want to come with you too.'

Vinay laughed at Payal and said, 'We will go together to Mumbai. Don't worry.'

Payal said, 'Promise?!'

'Yes, promise,' Vinay said.

Mother said, 'Where had you gone after all?'

Vinay said, 'I had gone to meet my friends, and then we had planned to go to the lake so we had gone there. I have called my friends in evening. I have organised a party tonight, Mother.'

His mother said, 'This is very good, my son. We haven't had a party in this house for many days. Without you, even I didn't celebrate any festival properly.'

Then Raja, Vinay, and Jaya started to make arrangements for the party. And after some time, Jai and Archit also came. They also helped them. All of Vinay's friends came in this party. And in some time, music also started. Everybody started to dance to the music.

Vinay said, 'What an enjoyable moment! We were so bored in Mumbai, and there is this unique feeling here.'

Jaya said, 'Yes, you are right.'

Vinay introduced Jaya to his friends. Vinay's friend said, 'Vinay, you have married that girl you chose in college on stage. We still remember that.'

Vinay laughed at this. He said, 'What should I tell you? My love has a very unique story.'

Then everybody said, 'Please tell that story. What is your love story?'

Vinay said, 'If I start narrating the story, this party will stop here.'

Then they said, 'OK, next time definitely tell us your love story.'

Vinay thought, 'Even I don't know Jaya's previous birth love story. I asked my sweetheart, but she did not tell me.'

Everybody enjoyed the party. After having dinner, Vinay met everyone again and said to all, 'My friends, don't forget to each other in life. I have arranged this party to meet all of you. Without friends, this life is nothing.'

Jai said, 'We will remember you all life, but you don't forget us.'

Vinay said, 'I will never forget you, my dear friends.' They talked for some time, then they all left. After the friends went, it was like a desert. The sound man came and dismantled the sound system.

Vinay said to Jaya, 'See, Jaya, everybody has left us. I am feeling very bad. You don't leave me.'

Then they slept. The next day, Vinay had to go to Mumbai. The next day, he said to his mother, 'Be ready. We will go to Mumbai at two o'clock.'

His mother said, 'I will not come with you. What will I do there?'

Vinay said, 'Mother, even I don't like the city without you. I have come here to take you.'

Then his mother said, 'See, your father is not well since last month, so I have to stay here with him.'

Then Vinay's father came and said, 'Vinay is saying again and again, then why you are not ready to go?'

Vinay said, 'One thing is possible if, Father, you too come with us?'

Then he said, 'I cannot come there. I have to manage the shop. Raja will look after the home.'

'OK, Father, I am going with Mom.' Then she was ready to go after being told again and again by Vinay. Vinay, Jaya, and his mother got ready to go to Mumbai. But Payal's face became sad.

She came to Vinay and said, 'Uncle, you had promised me, do you remember?'

Then Vinay said, 'Yes, I remember that I promised. You are coming with me to Mumbai. But first you ask your mother. After that, we will go to Mumbai.'

As told by Vinay, she went to her mother and asked her, 'I want to go with Uncle to Mumbai.'

His mother said, 'Have you gone mad? You don't know your exam is starting from tenth and you are going to Mumbai with your uncle. You will fail, and then you will realise. Now you are in third class. And I cannot make you understand again and again. So do as you wish.'

Payal thought, 'I should go in summer vacation.'

Payal came to Vinay and said, 'My exam is starting from tenth. So I will come in summer vacation.'

Vinay said, 'OK, you pay attention to your studies.'

Payal said, 'Please bring a bicycle for me.'

'OK, I will definitely bring a bicycle for you, Payal. OK, bye.'

Then they left for Mumbai. His mother said, 'I don't like hotel food. I brought home-made food with me.

Vinay said, 'This is very good. We will get the chance of having home-made food again.'

His mother said, 'The journey is very long. On the way, you will be tired, then take rest.'

'Yes, you are right. I will be tired, then Jaya will drive the car.'

The next day, they reached Mumbai. Due to it being a long journey, they rested. Then his mother said to Vinay, 'Don't go to office tomorrow. You are tired today.'

'Yes, Mother, you right. I don't want to go to office tomorrow too. I will start from day after tomorrow.'

Vinay informed his boss that he would resume work from the day after the next day.

In the evening, his mother, Jaya, and Vinay were talking; during their conversation, his mother talked to him about his family. 'My son, we have done a lot of struggle in life.' Then she started telling tales about Vinay's father. 'Your father was like an orphan. He was brought up by your aunt (your father sister).

'When your father was five years old, his parents died. Your aunt, (your father's sister), went to work every day and earned money for managing their home. That time, your father and aunt were facing problem of poverty. Your aunt took care of your father because your father was small. They faced starvation. Your aunt was very diligent. She sent your father to school. Your father didn't like to study. So he said to your aunt, "I won't go to school now. All my friends are earning and I am wasting time here going to school." Then your aunt thought, "Dilip is right. If we both start to earn all our debts will be paid. But if Dilip will not study, how will he become a good man?"

'Then your aunt said, "You have to go to school. It is clear. I don't want to spoil your future. I will pay all debts."

'Then your father suggested, "OK, I will do part time job after classes." Your father wanted to do effort because his sister was struggling quite a lot in life, so he thought, "If I will not support my sister, then who else will support her?"

'She asked, "But what will you do?"

'Your father replied, "My friend said to me that if I will do job in his shop he will pay five hundred rupees per month."

'Your aunt said, "You will work in his shop. It is not better. I will open a shop for you."

"But from where will you bring money for opening new shop, my sister?"

'Then she said, "You have given me scholarship money."

'Your father said, "But I have given that only for your dress. Why didn't you buy a dress for yourself? This is not fair."

'Then your aunt said, "I will buy a dress when you will earn from the shop."

'Your father said, "It is too less for shop. I need six hundred rupees for a juice machine. I want to open a juice shop.

'Then she said, "Don't worry. I will bring from where I am working."

'After a few days, your father opened a juice shop. After school, he sold juice. This shop became a success. Your father would even study in shop and sleep in shop. He earned more money than your aunt.

'But still your aunt did a job. They were in debts. Gradually, your father's income increased. Then he started earning two thousand rupees per month. Your father collected money and got your aunt married.

'After some days, your father opened a shop for garments. Then your father married me. When I came, your father's status was not so well. He had to pay all debts of our marriage. So I started stitching clothes, but it was not a success. Your father told me, "You don't have to do work till I am live." Then your father finally opened a shop of electronics, so today we have reached this state.'

Vinay said, 'Father and you have done a great job, Mom. But where is my aunt?'

Vinay's mother said, 'What can I tell you? She is not in this world now. The next month after my marriage, your aunt gave birth to a baby, but she died and said her last byes to her four sons and daughter and us. After some days, the baby also died, whom your aunt had left in this world.'

Vinay said, 'My aunt was great. She had done a great job. We do not find such people in this world. We have to remember her as she had done a lot of hard work.'

Then it was midnight, so they slept. The next day, they went shopping with his mother. Jaya and Vinay's mom purchased some clothes for her and also for Vinay. After this, Vinay took his mother to Sai Mandir. There they sat in mediation. Jaya said to Vinay's mother, 'In this temple, it is very peaceful. You will realise it. Please close your eyes.' After mediation, they came back home.

The next day, Vinay had to go to office; he got up early in the morning and started his usual daily jobs.

# 25

# Engagement of Tara and Jai, Salim Gets Job

Over there, Tara's love became somewhat less for Vinay. She thought, 'Now thinking about Vinay is useless.' But she could not forget Vinay. She still looked at Vinay's picture sometimes. Her father tried to make her understand.

'Till when will you remember Vinay? You don't know he has gone so far away from you.'

She said, 'A lamp of Vinay's love is in my heart and it will continue forever. Yes, I know it that he will not come back to me. But I cannot think about someone else. Don't trouble me for marriage. Do you want that I shouldn't stay with you in this home?'

'No, my daughter, what are you talking? Don't worry, my daughter. I will never say about marriage again.'

One day, Vinay made a call to Tara; her father picked up the phone. Vinay said, 'Good morning, Uncle.'

Tara's father replied to Vinay, 'After destroying my daughter's life, why are you making a call to us? What do you want now?'

Then Vinay said, 'Can I talk to Tara, Uncle? Please give the phone to Tara.'

After listening to Vinay's humble voice, Tara's father's heart melted; his intention changed.

Tara was very happy to know that Vinay had called her.

Vinay said, 'How are you, Tara?'

She said, 'You left me here lonely without you, and you are asking how I am?'

Vinay said, 'Please forgive me. And tell me one thing. Do you still love me as before?'

'Yes, Vinay, I love you still as before,' she said.

Vinay said, 'If you still love me, then you have to obey one thing.'

Tara said, 'I am ready to obey everything.'

Vinay said, 'OK, one of my friends is coming for engagement. He is a very good boy for you. He will change your life. He is a computer engineer. Don't refuse this proposal.'

She became silent for some time, then said, 'What are you saying, Vinay?' But she remembered that she had promised to Vinay that she would obey his order. She said, 'I will obey your order otherwise I will never forgive myself.'

She agreed to get married. As told by Vinay, Jai's family came to Tara's house to see Tara. Tara's father didn't know that they were sent by Vinay. First he thought, 'I will refuse them without meeting.' But he thought our Religion say that guests are equal to God. 'So we have to respect them always.'so he called him with respect.

Then guest came inside the home and talked with each other. Tara brought tea for the guests.

After seeing Tara, Jai's parents said, 'Your daughter is very beautiful. We like her.'

Jai too was happy to see Tara. He thought, 'What my friend Vinay had said to me was accurate—that I will never get a girl like Tara.'

Then Tara's father said, 'You have come here, this is very good for us, but my daughter is not ready for marriage.'

Jai's father thought, 'Are we at the wrong address?'

Then Jai's mother said, 'If your daughter is not ready to marry, no problem. But at least they should talk to each other one time.'

Tara's father said, 'OK, there is no problem in their meeting.'

They all went out from the guest room except Tara and Jai. Then their interview began in the guest room. Jai wanted to talk to Tara, but he felt shy and said, 'What is your name?' He knew her name, but he didn't know from where to start talking to this pretty girl.

Tara gave a smile to Jai and said, 'My name is Tara.' She too felt shy to talk with Jai.

Then Jai said, 'How do you find me?' Tara kept her eyes down and didn't reply to Jai. Jai thought, 'Maybe she doesn't like me.' The guest room became silent for a moment.

In this silent moment, Tara thought, 'Maybe he doesn't like me. So he is silent.' To break the silence, she asked Jai, 'What is your name?'

Hearing this sentence, Jai laughed and he said, 'My name is Jai.' Then they both smiled together. And in this smile they got the answer whether they liked or disliked each other.

Then jay's parent left. Tara's father said to Tara, 'If you are not ready for marriage, then why are you wasting the time of the guests and ours?

Then Tara replied, 'I like Jai.'

'So are you ready for marriage?'

Tara replied, 'Yes, Father, I am ready to marry Jai.'

Tara's father couldn't believe in this incident and that his daughter had said that she was ready for marriage. He wondered how this magic had happened on his daughter that she was ready for marriage. He said to himself, 'Thank God, you have changed my daughter's life.'

Tara and Jai got married with fanfare. Jai invited all his friends to his wedding; he also invited Vinay, but he could not come because of his office.

Jai and Tara's love grew with their marriage. Tara settled down in her new home with Jai. Gradually, she forgot her love for Vinay. After some days, Tara's father came to know that it was all done by Vinay. He realised that Vinay was not a bad man, and he was a hero. Due to circumstances, he could not marry his daughter. 'There is no fault of Vinay. I was wrong, when I was thinking about Vinay to be so bad.' Tara's father ended his rift with Vinay. He thought about God. 'We have to only trust in God, then all work will be done by God. Only trust can solve any problem.'

Jaya's sister, Rukhsar, was managing her expense with the money sent by her sister. From childhood, she had lived with her sister Jaya and their father, Ashif

Khan. As they were poor, they both sister couldn't study. Rukhsar was just like Jaya Khan. They have the same personality. Anjum had wanted to marry Jaya Khan. But his dream was not fulfilled. Finally, he came to know that Aslam's name was Vinay. He thought, 'He had cheated me.' After Jaya Khan, his eyes fell on Rukhsar. He told Rukhsar, 'I like you.' But she went to her aunt's home without answering Anjum.

Rukhsar and Jaya's aunt knew that there was no one belong to Jaya and Rukhsar except me after their father died, I have to take care of her. But her aunt was still very angry with the marriage of Jaya Khan. But when Rukhsar and Salim's engagement was done, she felt she could breathe easily; she was comforted.

Salim got married to Rukhsar. Rukhsar accepted nikah with Salim; they got married. And she settled down with Salim.

Now Rukhsar come back his own house from his aunt home.because she was living with her aunt after Jaya khan married

The company where Salim was working closed, so their income stopped. They faced many problems due to unemployment. Salim said to her wife, 'You are facing problems because you married me.' He said, 'Please forgive me. I couldn't give you all happiness.'

Rukhsar said, 'Why are you feeling guilty? That is not your fault. Allah made us human beings. We should trust him. At some time, God will definitely listen to us.'

She made a call to her sister Jaya Khan without hesitation. She said, 'Didi (sister), how are you?'

Jaya said, 'I am fine, but how are you, my lovely sister?'

'I am not OK, Didi (sister).'

Jaya said, 'What happened? Don't worry I have sent you a money order. You will get it within five days.'

'Rukhsar said Didi (sister), I didn't inform you. Our aunt got me married with Salim. I wanted to call you, but Aunt is not happy with you. She is still angry with your marriage, so I did not call you, but right now Salim need job as soon as. Speak to Vinay about a job for Salim.'

Jaya said, 'It is very good news that you got married. I was worried about you that when will you get married, but by Allah's blessing everything became good. Rukhsar, I am very happy today. I will talk to Vinay about Salim's job.take care yourself

Ok didi (sister) bye bye'

In the evening, Vinay came back home from his office. Jaya said, 'I had worries about that matter. God has fulfilled my wish.'

Vinay said, 'I think you are talking about Rukhsar's marriage.'

'Yes, Vinay, I am talking about her. You are so talented you got my point. Once I heard about her marriage, I was very happy.'

'So tell me, how is my sister-in-law?'

Then Jaya said, 'It is very good that she got married, but the boy is from a poor family. His name is Salim. Please, you have to arrange a job for him.'

Vinay said, 'Why not? You can call him Mumbai. I will definitely do something for him, because I too have passed such a time and I had searched for a job like him. I can understand him'

The next day, Jaya made a call to Rukhsar and said, 'come Mumbai Both of you. Vinay has called both of you.'

But Rukhsar said, 'What will I do there? I am sending Salim. First Salim will settle, then I will think of coming.'

Jaya said, 'You are my sister. Don't talk like that. Come to me here. I want to meet you.' Then Rukhsar and salim came to Mumbai. Vinay met Salim and Rukhsar and asked about their marriage.

Rukhsar said, 'It was good, but you were not there.'

'So you should have called us.'

Then Rukhsar said, 'Because of yours and Jaya's marriage my aunt is angry. So I had not invited you. Oh, I am sorry.'

Then they talked among themselves. After having dinner, Vinay asked to Salim, 'Are you educated?'

Salim said, 'I have studied till class five. But I know driving and I have a drive license too.'

'Then I will get you a new taxi. How is my idea?'

Salim said, 'It is a very good idea, Vinay sir.' The next day, he got a taxi for Salim. And Vinay gave them a room near the parking of his flat.

Salim and Rukhsar started their life happily. After some days, Salim got a job in a good business line. And he took a room on rent near Vinay's flat and gradually his income increased.

Rukhsar said to Salim, 'See, Salim, I told you that Allah listens to everyone. Only you need to trust in him. Seeing Rukhsar's life, Jaya felt good that her sister was now good and well.

Then Vinay said to his mother, 'By your grace, everything good has happened.' Now all worries of Vinay were over after Rukhsar's settlement.

# 26

# Turn in Story

But this story takes a turn from here. A forty-five-year-old woman whose name was Janki lived near Vinay's village. She would always ask her husband, 'Where is my son? Where is my son? Where have you left my son in blind drinking of wine?'

Then her husband Badriprasad said, 'I had gone to buy wine. I told your son to sit there and that I was coming, but when I came back there he was not there. I was mad at that time. Please forgive me, Janki. Our baby is lost because of me.'

Janki and Badriprasad were husband and wife. They had six sons and the seven one was lost in childhood. Badriprasad had no sense because he had have wine that time. He lost his son.

From that day, Badriprasad felt regret for the child he had lost. From that time till now, Badriprasad had not touched wine or seen wine.

Due to this incident, people had changed their way of thinking and sacrificed wine for a lifetime of that village. And they all considered themselves responsible that Badriprasad lost his child.

Badriprasad had six sons, so he wanted a daughter, but this time too his wife birth a son instead of daughter.

They kept his name chhotu because he was small among his brother so everybody called him chhotu.

But Badriprasad became angry and started consuming wine because of this. One day, Badriprasad was about to go to a wine shop to buy wine. Chhotu started to pester him, 'I want to come with you too.' Badriprasad did not allow him to come with him, but Chhotu did not obey his father. Finally Badriprasad took him along.

On reaching the shop, he said to Chhotu, 'Please be seated here. I am coming.' Then Badriprasad left him there and started having wine. And as usual, he started to gamble with his friends. While gambling, he forgot that he had brought Chhotu with him. Then he realised that he had made a mistake. Then he remembered where he had left him. Then he went there where he had left him. But he couldn't found Chhotu. He came back home and told his wife, 'I have lost our small son, Chhotu.' On hearing this, Janki lost her head.

She said, 'Where has my son gone?' And his big brothers went to search for him; they searched for Chhotu the full night. But they couldn't find out where Chhotu was. They even searched for him for three to four days. But they couldn't find them.

Because they were poor, Badriprasad couldn't educate his sons. He had worked and fed them. His sons were unemployed as they were uneducated. But they had to work in place of studies.

Badriprasad wept the full night. He was thinking about their son. And he regretted, 'I am only the reason for my son getting lost.' After some days, Badriprasad died. Janki and her six sons started running their lives by waged and gradually improved their family status. Janki got all her sons married. But from here, Janki's bad days started. After marriage, the sons divided all the wealth among them and left Janki nothing. They didn't take care of their mother; they didn't even give medicine to their mother.

After this, she struggled with life, and even at this age, she went to wage and feed herself. Her sons didn't ask her as to how she was; she passed her life in such poverty.

On the other hand, Vinay started his album heartily. He always said to his friends, 'If you don't do work with inside, then your job will not be a success after all. If you want success, then you have to start every work with inside. I know that there are many troubles in the way of life. But you have to keep in mind your destiny every time. If you see a dream, then don't see it while sleeping. But if you wake up due to that dream, then it will not take much time to successfully remember this.'

Vinay's friends learnt from Vinay about moral life. They gave support to Vinay with full effort, so his album became hits. And Vinay too become famous.

Vinay knew that intoxication, dope, fix, narcotic, soup (smoking wine) is taking many people's lives. He doesn't like cigarette weed.

He hates those who sell such thing.

His opinion was that the government should stop such companies that made such injurious health items.

He sent a complaint to the government office, but no action was taken by the government.

So he wrote a song on smokers so that people left all dope and drugs.

*Where in hand smoke in pocket cigarette . . .*

After listening to this song, many people left smoking and drinking, smoking tobacco, etc. And people gave honour to Vinay. Now his name was on the list of top ten singers. But due to this success, some people became jealous with Vinay as they had lost their business because of Vinay's success, who belonged to music companies. They made a plan about Vinay who has ruined their business. They even gave him an offer to work with them, but Vinay refused to work with them. Now if Vinay continued to sing, then their company would close down, so they hired a man was a killer and gave him fifty million to kill Vinay.

Vinay didn't know this. But Jaya realised that it would soon be likely. So she said to Vinay, 'You take care. This world is not good. I had lost you one time. I don't want to again lose you.'

Vinay said, 'Life and death is in hands of God. In this, we cannot change anything. Whatever will happen will definitely happen. Nobody can change it. God is driving our life and he can stop it when he wants to.

'You are right, but at least we should be alert.'

Jaya loved Vinay very much; she wanted to be with Vinay all the time. So she said to Vinay, 'I want to come with you to office.'

Vinay said, 'This is very good. You should come with me and learn something there.' She started to go with Vinay to the studio.

Now people knew that she was Vinay's wife. Vinay's friends asked, 'How did you get married? Love or Arranged?'

Vinay said, 'Jaya is my lover not only from this birth, but she was with me in previous birth.'

His friends said, 'How can this possible?'

Vinay said, 'This is right.' They knew that they were lovers of previous birth. And Jaya had remembered her previous birth.

On hearing this, his film director wanted to know the story and he wanted to make a film on this story. The director asked Jaya, 'Please give me this story. We want to make a movie on this.'

Jaya replied to him, 'I will reply to you later.'

Then Jaya came back home and said to Vinay, 'That director was asking me for our love story. You tell me what should we do?'

Vinay replied to Jaya, 'Not now. This story is not complete still.'

On hearing this, she felt uneasy. She said, 'I am feeling that something will go wrong.'

Vinay said, 'You are right, but don't worry. We will always be with each other, I am sure.'

Jaya said, 'Don't leave me. Otherwise I will die.'

# 27

# Secret of Vinay's Life

Khushilal who was a friend of Badriprasad knew the secrets of the child whom Badriprasad had lost. Khushilal also knew who had taken that small boy of Badriprasad from near the wine shop that night. He hadn't informed about this secret to his family; he knew that where the boy would stay was a rich man's house, and he would take care of him properly. The man who had taken the child would educate him, because Badriprasad was a poor man and he could not take care of the boy properly. So Khushilal didn't inform about this secret to anyone.

But now the time had come to inform his mother the where abouts of her son. She had been waiting for her son since many years.

Then Khushilal went to Badriprasad's home to inform the secret of the lost child to his mother. He knocked at the door. Janki opened the door. She said, 'Brother, after many days you have come here.'

He said, 'I was busy in some work. Tell me how you are.'

She said, 'What should I say to you? My own sons are not helping me. If I ask for money for medicine, they say to me in this dire situation it is difficult to eat food and you are asking for money. They don't even come to me now. Oh God, what has happened to them?'

Khushilal said, 'Don't worry. Trust in God. He helps everyone.'

'OK, please now tell me what can I do for you? What have you come here for?'

'I came here to meet you, and I want to tell you something special.'

'Then tell me.'

He said, 'Twenty years have passed. I am talking about that black night. My friend, Badriprasad, your husband, had forgotten about the child and gone to the wine shop and started gambling.

'That time I was passing through that road and I saw that Mr Dilip Shrivastav and his wife had taken the child. I am sure that was your son. And he must be a very good man now. That time I didn't inform this to anyone. I have kept this secret because I knew at that time your family was very poor. You couldn't bring up your son. So your sons were doing wages. So I felt that hiding this secret is a better way to make that child's life.'

As soon as she heard this, Janki became very excited to know that her son was live. 'I have passed this life in search of him. I got him now.'

She thanked Khushilal and said, 'Today you have given me a hope to live life.'

After knowing about her child, Janki went to Mr Dilip Shrivastav's house to search for her child and she begged to meet her son.

Then Raja Bhaiya (Vinay's brother) said to Janki, 'Who is your son? You are talking about that son whom you couldn't take care in childhood and lost him on the road. You cannot care for a child, then why did you give birth? Go away from here. We don't have your son.' After saying this, he shut the door.

The next day, he opened the door. He found that the old woman (Janki) was still at the gate. Then Raja became mad. He lost his head. He thought, 'What have I done? She is asking for her own son. Not only this, but she is also mother of Vinay Shrivastav, who is making their family name famous. If something were to happen to the old woman in such a cold night, then I will give an answer to Vinay.' Then Raja said to Janki, 'Please forgive me. I have made a mistake. Your son, Vinay, is in Mumbai. Now he is a great singer.' Raja behaved with her as if she was his own mother and got food for her to eat.

After taking information about her son, she came back to her home. Janki said to her sons, 'Your younger brother is alive, whom we had lost in childhood. The son of Dilip Shrivastav is your brother.'

Vinay's brothers were not much happy to hear this news. They said to Janki, 'You have informed us, this is good. This is good news for us. We will go to meet him. You have done good that you didn't bring him here. Otherwise you know how we are living. He cannot stay here one night.'

They understood that one more division in the wealth would happen if he will to come there.

Then her mother said, 'I am going to bring him. You arrange some money for me.' As soon as she asked for money, they all become silent.

They said, 'What will you do after bringing him here? Don't bring him here. He is good where he is now.'

Janki asked her son for money, but no one was ready to give money to her. Finally, she knew that he would not give money to her. Then she went to Khushilal and said, 'You have done favour for me. I want one more help from you. Give me some money so that I can meet my son.'

Khushilal was also a poor man. So he refused to give her money. But he thought, 'There is no meaning if I have informed her about her son and I do not arrange money for her.'

Then Khushilal said, 'How much you need?'

She said, 'I have to go to Mumbai. I don't know how much is charged for fare.'

Khushilal said, 'Two thousand rupees is enough for fare.' Then he went to the banker of the village and asked for money.

The banker said to Khushilal, 'What you have as a grantee so I can give you money on behalf of that.

Then Khushilal said to the banker, 'I need this money for Janki. She is going to meet her son at Mumbai and she will bring money from there.' 'then I will pay you.

On Khushilal's request, the banker was ready to give money.

'But banker said if I do not get my money, then I will make you my slave. Until you pay all debts, you have to stay here as my slave.'

Khushilal said, 'I agree with you. As you say, I will do.' Then the banker brought money and gave it to Khushilal, and Khushilal gave this money to Janki.

Janki touched the money to her head and said, 'God, please help me.' She was glad to get the money. She thought, 'How will I meet my son?'

Now she knew that her son was a very rich man. After arranging money, she started on her journey to Mumbai to meet her son Vinay. On the third day, she reached Mumbai. She started to search for Vinay. She asked everyone about her son and where was Vinay's house. On hearing this, some people made fun of her. Even then, she was not ready to accept defeat; she had to search for her son. But she thought, 'How will I recognise him? I have forgotten his face. When he was five, I had seen him.' Even then she continued to search. Finally, she met an honest man. She said to him, 'Vinay is my son and I came here to meet him.'

The man thought for a moment, 'The old woman has gone crazy.' Then he said, 'You are making up a very good story. I know this as Vinay's mother is staying with him for the last two years.' Then Janki narrated to him the story about her son.

Then he asked Janki, 'He knows that you are his mother?'

She said, 'He was five years old when he got lost.'

'Then he will never meet you, because he is a famous man. He will not talk to you even. Do one thing. Go back home. You will not get to meet him.'

Then Janki said, 'Why will I go back? I came here with hope after taking borrowed money.'

'But there is no meaning. He doesn't know you and you don't know him. How will you both meet each other? It will be very difficult for you to meet.

Even after this, there was no effect on her hope and belief. Janki went to Vinay's house and said to the gatekeeper, 'Vinay is my son. And I am his mother.'

Then the gatekeeper drove her away. But Janki was stubborn. Then the gatekeeper said, 'This scene is just like in movies. This cannot be real. Please go away. I have to do my job. If you want to meet him, I can note your appointment. But if you are speaking a lie at such an age I will feel very bad.'

# 28

# Vinay Meets His Real Mother

Janki was still waiting for her son. Then Vinay came in his car. On seeing the big car, she realised that it must be her son. Once his car went inside the gates, she cried loudly, 'Son, I am your mother.' Vinay felt for a moment as if his real mother was calling him. He stopped the car and got out of the car.

He asked Janki, 'Who are you?'

She replied to Vinay, 'I am your mother. You are my son, and you are asking me who I am?'

Then Janki narrated to him her story. Then Vinay realised that maybe she was right. Vinay said to her, 'Please come inside. Everything will be clear.'

His mother (not real) said after seeing the thirst in Janki's eyes, 'Yes, Vinay, she is right. She is your real mother.'

Vinay's eyes became tearful on seeing his mother in such a condition.

Janki also became sad and said, 'We lost you. We did not take care of you properly.'

Then Vinay said, 'How did I become lost, Mother? What is the reason that today I am here, my mother?'

Then Janki narrated to him the story about him. 'You have six brothers. They want to meet you. You are number seven. Your father wanted a daughter, but his wishes were not fulfilled. Then you were born. Due to this, he started to consume wine. And one day, due to your stubbornness, he took you with him. And this became very bad news for us and you lost

But he realised his fault. After this, he regretted his full life. He wanted to meet you his entire life. This was his last wish. But his last wish could not be completed. At his last moment, he spoke to me, "Whenever you get my child, say to him to please forgive me." So, my son, I am asking sorry from your father's side.'

Vinay now knew the strange story about his life. After listening to this painful story, his eyes became tearful. Jaya's heart became grief-stricken on listening to the story of Vinay.

Then Vinay said, 'Why did he ask for sorry? He has made my life. Who is saying that I am lost by him? He had sent me that time to my destiny. Whatever I am today, it's only because of him.

'God makes everyone's life as per their life's base. God have written my future in this way so Jaya and I met in this birth.

This is very great obligation. I am your indebted to you.'

Janki said, 'Now the thirst of my eyes is over now. My son, I have come here to take you back, but this is not my right to take you with me because your mother is like a goddess who has brought you up and made your life. Vinay, my son, don't forget me. Now I have to go.'

Vinay said, 'No, Mother, you will stay with us from today.'

Janki said, 'No, my son, my grandson is waiting for me.'

Vinay asked his mother again and again to stay with him, but she wasn't ready to stay there. Vinay became sad. Vinay sent some baggage with his mother. He said to his mother, 'Distribute these sweets and baggage among my brothers.' Vinay had kept fifty million rupees in a box of sweets without informing his mother.

The next day, the people came to know that Vinay was the son of a poor woman whose name was Janki; she was Vinay's real mother. Jaya too knew this strange story of her lover.

Then Vinay's mother said, 'Janki is a very great woman. She has given birth to you. And I got you. I am too lucky.'

Gradually, Vinay's album became a super hit. Vinay's company earned a lot of money and became very famous because of Vinay's album. Vinay too showed that he was a very good artist. But this success became bad luck for him. Some company owners made Vinay their enemy and resents his success. Vinay had completed seventy albums. All of them became super hits. He became a very rich man.

Vinay sent his real mother to her village by his car. His brothers were waiting for her and thinking, 'When will our mother come?' Then they saw that their mother had come. They were glad. Many people gathered to see Janki and the car because a car had come for the first time in that village. And when she got off the car, everybody's eyes were on her. They thought that she must have brought a lot of money with herself. Everybody was happy to know that her son was a rich man in Mumbai. Janki didn't know that Vinay had kept fifty million rupees in a packet of sweets. Then Janki went to her sons. They had thought, 'Our mother will be bringing some money, so our life will be easy for some days.'

Finally, they asked their mother, 'What did you bring, Mother?

She said, 'I brought some sweets and dry food.'

Hearing this, her elder son became angry and said, 'You had gone to bring for us only sweet? And you brought nothing else?'

She said, 'Yes, my son.'

They became sad to know that. 'OK, we will make do with these sweets.' When they opened the sweet packet, their expression changed in such way that does not happen in real life.they seemed that they are in dream. After seeing the lot of money, they all became very happy. Then they realised that their brother was a very good person. They distributed all the money among themselves and started their own business. They returned the money of the banker. They started their life. But they wanted to meet the real hero who had changed their lives. 'When will he come here?' They carried on with their lives, but Janki's health was not good now. She wanted to meet her son, Vinay, one more time.

# 29

# Vinay's Real Mother Is No More

One day, Vinay got a very bad dream. He said to Jaya, 'Today I got a bad dream about my mother, Janki. She is not well.'

Then Vinay's mother (stepmother) said to Vinay, 'Go and meet her. You know she came here to meet you without an address at such an age, but you didn't go there till now.'

'Yes, Mother, you are right. But what should I do? My job does not allow me. I have a lot of work. I will talk tomorrow in office for leave. We will leave tomorrow.'

Then Vinay left for office. He was busy in the office when he got a call from his mother Janki. He got the news that she was not well now. He came back home immediately. He drove to Janki's village with Jaya and his mother.

The next day he reached Janki's village. He met his mother. After seeing his mother in such a condition, he thought deeply. He said to his real mother Janki, 'I have come, Mother. I am your son, Vinay.'

She was happy to see Vinay. She said, 'My eyes have been starving for you.'

Vinay was glad to meet his brothers. His brothers were also glad to meet Vinay. They thought that their life changer was a good-natured man, who was their brother.

Vinay said to his brothers, 'Why don't you take care of Mother. See, Mother's heath is so bad. You all are responsible for her health. If you don't take care of Mother, then who will take care of Mother?'

Vinay's brothers said, 'Please forgive us. We haven't taken care of Mother. We were selfish. But when you sent money for us, then we realised that we were wrong. You are a very good man.'

Vinay couldn't stand to see his mother's situation; he said to his mother, 'Mother, don't worry. You will get well.' Vinay arranged for a good doctor for his mother. After treatment, there was still no improvement in her health. Vinay's mother (stepmother) and Jaya became very sad to see the health of his mother Janki.

Then Janki called her son Vinay to her (Janki wanted Vinay to come to her); she said to Vinay, 'I wanted to see you, Vinay. I made a call to you and you came here. My heart is satisfied now. My son whom I had lost in childhood, today he is in front of my eyes.' She said, 'Vinay, forgive me and your father. Your father was quite disturbed when you were lost. His last words were, "When you get my child, say to him please forgive me."'

On hearing this, Vinay's eyes become tearful. Vinay's stepmother also felt this grief for Janki.

Janki said to Jaya, 'Come to me, my daughter. Now I am going. You will give birth to a child, then love them from my side. I will not see my grandson, but you take care of them. Don't quarrel with Vinay. Don't make my son angry.'

Vinay said, 'Mom, you will be well. Don't talk like that.'

Then Janki said, 'My summons has come now. I have to go now.'

Vinay said, 'No, Mom, you don't leave us. I will not live without you.' She met all her grandsons and sons. After that, her soul left her body (she died). Vinay started to weep at her feet. His heart became very said. Vinay and his brothers performed manner of death. Vinay's elder brother offered fire to the bier. He performed all Sacrament.

Vinay eyes were showing her inside view. Now he realised what the grief of his mother going away was (disunion of his mother).

After some days, he came back to Mumbai. He said to his stepmother, what kind of game is this that i couldn't stay with my real mother?

His mother said, 'Yes, Vinay, God gave birth to us. And God made our life. Live this life with full enjoyment until your breath is running. Life and death are in the hands of God. I and you cannot change it. So forget everything and start again your life.'

After listening to his mother, his sadness became somewhat less. Staying with his mother and Jaya, he forgot the grief of his mother Janki's death.

He didn't go to office for some days. In his office, they knew about this incident, so they didn't call Vinay.

After some days, his brother Raja came to Mumbai. Vinay met his brother. He said to him that his mother Janki was no more. He requested his brother, 'Raja Bhaiya, please stay here for some days. I will show you Mumbai.'

Raja said, 'I came here to take Mother. Father is not well and Payal too cannot stay away from her grandma for such a long time.'

When he heard this, he felt grief that his father was not well. Then he made a call to his father, Mr Dilip Shrivastav. Vinay asked him, 'How are you?'

His father said, 'I am good. My sons, don't worry about me. Raja has come to Mumbai to take his mother. So send her to me.'

Vinay said, 'OK, I will send her to you, OK?'

Vinay felt grief as he had kept his mother away r from Payal, Raja Bhaiya, and his father. 'I have done this mistake. I have given punishment to them for my own happiness. They have every right to live with Mother after all.' Vinay said to his brother, 'Please forgive me, Brother. Due to me, Father is not well. If Mother were at home, she would have taken care of Father properly. And he would not have become unwell.'

After this, he asked about his father's business. Raja said, 'Everything is well, but Mother is absent. So I came here to take her.'

The next day, mother was gone with Raja Bhaiya to the village. After Mother had gone, his condition became very bad, because earlier his real mother had died and he could not forget it. And now his mother (stepmother) had also gone back to the village. Now Vinay had only Jaya to support him as such. Now he was not feeling good. He thought, 'My mother had given me confidence. And now she is not here.'

Jaya said, 'This home has become lonely without Mother.'

Vinay said you are right Jaya.

That side, Salim's business was now growing. Now he belonged to a middle class family. Salim had a new car also. One day, Salim and Rukhsar came to Vinay's home with sweets. Jaya and Vinay were very happy to see Salim and Rukhsar. They said, 'What happened? You are coming here after a long time.'

Salim said, i was busy because of business so we came after long time, sir. Today whatever we have is a blessing of you. Vinay sir, you are a very good person.'

Jaya met her sister. After meeting Salim and Rukhsar, Vinay's tension reduced now.

After having dinner, Rukhsar said to Vinay, 'You should come to our small home.'

Vinay said, 'Surely we will come to your home sometime.'

Salim said, 'Rukhsar, we should leave now. If we will stay some more time, then we will be late.'

Vinay said, 'Don't go now, and it is already late at night. Stay here now.'

On Vinay's insistence, they stayed there that night.

In the night, Salim and Vinay talked to each other. And on the other side, Jaya and Rukhsar started their story separate.

Vinay asked Salim, 'What is your father's occupation in the village?'

Salim said, 'Vinay sir, my uncle hasn't help us as much as you helped us. My father and my uncle have equal property of their father's wealth, as is in every family rule. My father got his part. And my uncle got his part of wealth. For some days our family's condition was good. But my mother had cancer. For a long time, she was suffering from this disease. Some days before Ramzan she lost this fight. She said to us a last bye. She was gone. Then our home was dismissed. We had taken money from my uncle for treatment of my mother.

'That time, our condition became very bad. We couldn't pay the debts of my uncle. By grace of God, I started driving a van. But that time was very bad for us. We were again unsuccessful. My uncle took my field for the debt money. And after some days my father died too. I became lonely. I feared about my life and what would happen to my life. But Allah listened to my voice. I felt that I had to do a job. So I started a job in the company and managed my expense. I didn't think about my uncle that he could do so. He had taken all my property and got it signed by me. But At Allah's house, it can be dealy, but not despair. Allah sent an angel in my life. She was Rukhsar. Rukhsar worked there, where I was working. One day, I proposed to Rukhsar for a love marriage. And her aunt too wanted that she should get married as soon as possible. She

wanted that Rukhsar should get a good husband.
I was in her fate. Finally by Allah's grace, we had our
wedding.'

After listening to Salim's story, Vinay thought
deeply. He said, 'Salim, God will help everyone. In this,
there is no contribution of me and you.

Vinay said oh salim If you don't have a T V, then
take T V from here. It is useless here.'

Salim said, 'We owe a lot of obligation to you. Now
I don't want to take anything more. First I will pay this.'

Vinay said, 'Don't say this again. I consider you as
my family and you are talking like that. Take this T V
with you without informing me tomorrow, positively.'

Salim said, 'I agree.'

Vinay said, 'My real mother died some days before.
Now I am very upset due to my mom. I am not feeling
well. I don't want to go to office. But I have to go to
office tomorrow after a long leave.

Salim said, 'Don't worry, Vinay. It's all done by
god. But you should forget everything. Start your work
heartily,'pay attentation on your work. You will forget
every thing

Vinay said, 'You are right, but my heart cannot
understand this.'

Then Vinay and Salim went to sleep in the night.

The next day in the morning, Vinay said, 'I will
drop you at your home. Take this TV.'

Then Vinay dropped them at their home. And he
went to his office After a long period, all were happy to
see Vinay.

# 30

# Vinay's Album Is Hit and Someone Plans to Kill Him

At the office, everybody was waiting for Vinay. Because of Vinay's absence, his seven albums were pending. He thought, 'Due to my absence my boss has suffered loss in the company.'

He apologised to his boss and said, 'I will finish this pending work in a few days.'

Vinay called his team and explained to them. 'Now our work is so pending. So we have to handle this and coordinate with each other.' Then they started to work day and night. They finished their pending job in a month only. Vinay's new album came in the market. They all were super hit. Because of this new album, Vinay came again in the top ten list of singers.

His boss arranged a party for Vinay because he had finished all pending work only in a month. Vinay and his team and Jaya also came to this party.

His boss said to Vinay, 'Vinay, well done. You have done this job in few days, after doing full effort day and night. I am very happy with you.'

I can't take all the credit for all this work. This is a contribution of all team members. They support me every time.

His boss thanked to all who sport every time Vinay.

His boss was already talking with Jaya. He thought that their love story was unique. And some days before, he had said to Jaya, 'I need movie scripts for films. So you give me your love story.' He said again to Vinay, 'I want to make a movie on your love story.'

Vinay refused him and said, 'You already asked Jaya about this topic. We have denied to give the story.'

After listening to these words, he got angry on Vinay. He said to Vinay, 'Have you gone mad, Vinay? I will pay whatever you need. And you are refusing again and again. What do you think of yourself?'

Vinay said, 'Now you are drunk. We will talk about this tomorrow.' But his boss did not listen to him.

His boss said, 'You have reached your destiny only because of me. And today you are refusing me for story. If I want, I can destroy your career in a minute.'

Vinay didn't reply to his boss. Hearing Vinay's boss's words, Jaya said to Vinay, 'Let's go, Vinay. I know today that your boss is a very cheap man.' Because of this quarrel, everybody left the party. Nobody stayed there. All people had gone without having dinner.

On seeing this, his boss regretted it. 'What a mistake I have done. I am a very cheap man. For my own needs, I have disturbed all. I shouldn't have done this.'

Jaya said to Vinay, 'Your boss is a very selfish man.'

Vinay explained to her, 'No, Jaya, he is a very good man. He was drunk so he had no sense and spoke rude words. He is a very good person in ordinary life. You see, Jaya, he will definitely apologise for this incident. You don't worry about him. I know him very well.'

Vinay didn't feel angry after hearing his boss's rude words because he knew that nobody could be so bad. He had done that because of circumstances. Vinay forgot that and slept.

In the morning, he got up and saw his mobile, then he was surprised. He thought, 'Ten missed calls from the boss in the night. What happened?' He made called him back and said, 'What is the matter?'

His boss replied, 'Vinay, please forgive me. I made a mistake in the night.'

Vinay said, 'Sir, I have forgotten that.'

He also apolized to team member who were present in that parti.

His boss felt guilty. He knew that Vinay was a very good man and would forgive him. 'After saying such bad things in the night, he is not angry with me. Really, he is a diamond.'

After some days, Vinay got a call from his hometown. 'My son, come back. We want to meet.'

Vinay said to his mother, 'Yes, Mother, we too always think about you.'

Payal said, 'Uncle, when will you come back? I am waiting for you.'

With everyone requesting him to come, he made a plan to visit his hometown. Vinay said to Jaya, 'Tomorrow is Saturday. Do packing for tomorrow. Once I will come back from office, we will go to hometown.'

On hearing this plan, she made all preparations for the journey.

The next day he went to office and said to his boss, 'I need leave for a month to go to my hometown.'

On seeing Vinay's hard work he agreed to give him a leave from work for a month. Vinay got a chance to go home. Vinay came back home to Jaya after half day and they departed for his hometown.

On the way, they saw a beautiful temple and they stopped the car. They went towards the temple.

They entered inside the temple and they got unique peace there. Vinay and Jaya had a peaceful moment there, and they sat there for a while in a state of meditation. Soon they became thoughtless in that position. They realised their inside power. Vinay said to Jaya, 'We were wasting time in Mumbai, but the real joy is here.'

Jaya said, 'You are right.'

After some time, a priest came and asked them, 'What are you doing?'

Then Vinay said to the priest, 'We are enjoying the love of God.'

The priest laughed and said, 'We are staying here from a long time and doing worship to God. But we didn't realise love of God. And you are saying that you are enjoying the love of God.'

Jaya said to the priest, 'To get this state, first we have to forget ego, enemy, attachment, allure, and selfishness. We have to have pure desire to get God. We have to sacrifice all problems. We cannot connect with God with problems. And sitting here with thoughtless with awareness is the only way to the kingdom of God. Then you will realise it. If you are searching God with your problems and tension, then you will never get God. Don't make formalities with God. Do worship from inside. God has created this world and he knows how we remember and worship them. You forget all your problems, grief, pain and recognise your soul. If you know your life's moral values and enjoy your life with love of God, then you will definitely realise this power of God.'

After listening to Jaya, the priest thought, 'They are really my teacher. They are speaking reality. According to them, today I know I was wrong.'

After some time, Jaya and Vinay came out of the temple. Then they saw a row of beggar men. They prayed to God for the beggars and they gifted snacks and clothes to them.

# 31

# Final Meeting of Vinay

Vinay reached home with Jaya. They touched his parents' feet. Vinay's mother said, 'I am seeing you after a long time. My eyes were waiting for you.'

Vinay said, 'We too remember you, think about you.'

On seeing his car, Vinay said, 'My car is still there where I left it.'

'Yes, my son, she is also waiting for you and saying that when will my Vinay come. Nobody drives it after you shifted to Mumbai. And we used to remember about your study room, your toys, book and etcetera, these reminds us of your childhood story. However we think about you my son.

You childhood is in my eyes till now.'

Then Payal came fast and latched on to Vinay. 'You didn't bring my favourite. You forgot about me after going to Mumbai.'

Vinay said, 'I remember your favourite. How can I forget it?'

Jaya said, 'Now you are growing. Now your favourite dish will bring your husband.'

On listen to this, Payal's eyes became tearful. She felt that now she would have to go away from her uncle and parents after marriage.

Then Jaya said, 'Oh, Payal, I am just joking with you. And you became so sad.'

Meanwhile Raja Bhaiya also came. Vinay embraced his elder bother. After meeting Raja Bhaiya, he made a plan to arrange for a party that night, so he called his best friends: Archit, Lalita, Jai, and Tara.

In the night, the party started. Lalita said to Jai, 'Vinay is so smart. He arranged Archit to marry me to keep me away from himself.'

Tara said, 'Same here. He got me married off with Jai to keep me away from himself. Really, he is such a smart person.' All laughed at that.

Then Vinay said, 'This is right. Tara loved me very much and she was not ready to marry, so I thought her life would be destroyed if she didn't marry because of me. One day I asked her if she still loved me. She said yes. I asked her, "Will you obey me?" She said yes, then I said to her, "Please marry Jai." And she agreed to marry Jai. She is really a moral of love. God bless her.' Salim and Rukhsar too came in the party. They thought that the story of Vinay was so different. Jaya met her sister Rukhsar.

Vinay was glad to see all the people in the party. Vinay thought, 'I don't know, but I have a feeling that I am meeting with these people for the last time. I think I will not meet them the next time.' His face became somewhat sad. He sang a song for Tara and Lalita:

*This evening is very cheerful!*
*My greetings to all.*
*Fully enjoy this life.*
*Have this goblet.*
*This evening is very cheerful!*
*Come and embrace me, my friends.*
*Sing this song all.*
*Don't trust on life.*
*Live with full enjoyment.*
*There is no grief in our life.*
*This evening is very cheerful!*
*Life is very small.*
*And targets are lot of.*
*I feel like that*
*Where we start still we are there.*
*There is no rest in my life.*
*This evening is very cheerful!*

Everyone clapped for this song. They thought, 'The great singer is among us today.' Some people took photos of Vinay.

Vinay said to everyone, 'Have dinner.' After having dinner, they left for home. After some time, everybody was gone. Vinay felt his home was like a desert or as if someone had pushed him in a dark well. In such a moment, Vinay came to Jaya. He embraced her and said, 'You don't go away from me like my friends have gone.'

Jaya understood that Vinay knew about his future, so she said to Vinay, 'Don't worry. I will be with you for birth after birth.'

The next day he planned to go to the old temple. He said to Jaya, 'Come with me to the old temple, where you waited for me. I used to come to see you.'

Jaya said, 'I am ready. Let's go.' Then Jaya and Vinay reached the old temple. They cleared the garbage and leaves from the statue. After praying to God, he got some cut grass near the temple. He had repaired the temple; after clearing, the temple looked very beautiful. People also started to come to see God. Vinay felt good that the temple was looking very good now.

Vinay stayed for a long period in his village. After some days, he got ready to go to Mumbai.

He said to his mother, 'Get ready, Mother. We are going to Mumbai.'

Then his mother said, 'What will I do there? Now your father's health is not well. How can I come after leaving him here? I have to stay here to take care of him.'

'OK, we will take Father with us.'

But she refused to come to Mumbai. And said, 'Don't go to Mumbai and stay with us.'

Vinay said, 'I will come after some days, but one thing. You are not coming, no problem, but when I will call you, please come immediately.'

'OK, Vinay.'

Payal looked at Vinay in such a way as if her eyes were asking, 'I want to come too.' Vinay touched his father's feet. But he felt like that he would not stay there without his mother. Then he said to his mother, without you if I won't be stay there then what i will do?

His mother said, 'Why are you worrying about me? Jaya is also going with you. You are not lonely. Call me whenever you feel bad. Don't worry. We will come to you in Mumbai.'

Then Vinay was ready for go. But on seeing Payal's silent face, he thought that she wanted to come with him. Her face looked very lovely in this state. She said to Vinay, 'I want to come with you too.'

Vinay said, 'Go and ask your mother that I am going with Uncle. 'After taking permission from her mother, they got ready to go to Mumbai.

The next day, they reached Mumbai. Vinay thought that Payal would feel bad there because she had come so far away from her mother for the first time. So he bought some toys for her. Payal was pleased with Vinay and Jaya.

Jaya went to the market with Payal. They bought clothes for themselves.

On the way, Payal saw Shahrukh Khan. She became excited to see him; she said to Jaya, 'See, he is Shahrukh Khan.'

'Yes, Payal, this is Mumbai and heroes live here.'

Payal said to Jaya, 'Can I see Akshay Kumar too?'

Jaya said, 'Why not, but you have to wait for him?'

On the way, they had breakfast. And in the evening, they came home. But that day, the maid had not come. Then Payal said, 'I will cook food today.'

Then Jaya said, 'OK, we both will cook food today.' In the meantime, Vinay came.

After seeing her favourite dish in his hands, she said, 'You still bring favourite dish for me. Now I am a ten-year-old.'

Vinay laughed at Payal. He said, 'I have talked in a school for your admission. You will go to school in Vindya Mandir.'

Payal said, 'Uncle, I want to sing like you.'

Vinay said, 'First you have to study. Without study, there is nothing. We must study for everything, like singing, dancing, whatever.'

Then Payal started school.

The next day, Vinay's office was closed. Payal slept in her room. Vinay stayed with Jaya that day. Vinay said to Jaya, 'Can I love you?'

Then she smiled. 'What are you talking?'

Then Vinay said, 'At the time of our marriage, you felt shy even in talking. So I am asking you.' Vinay said to Jaya, 'Can I kiss you?'

She said, 'No, I feel shy.' However they reminded their old memory of love.

Vinay took Jaya in his arms. He realised that now this joyful life was going away from him. Vinay said to Jaya, 'I will leave you, then what will you do?'

Jaya said, 'Where will you go? Where you will go, I will be there Tara and Lalita left you, but I will not leave you.'

Vinay said, 'Please call my parents immediately.'

'Suddenly what happened to you? Please tell me clear why are you talking like that. Don't give me tension. Don't say a lie like this.

Vinay said, 'I want to meet my parents.'

Jaya's heart beat rapidly. She felt something was wrong. She made a call to Vinay's hometown. Jaya said, 'Vinay is not well. He is calling you.'

She called Vinay's parents there.

Payal said after seeing Vinay's face, 'Why are you nervous? I want to know why you are worrying.'

Then Vinay smiled and said, 'Who is in tension? I am seeing you in tension.'

Payal said, 'I won't go to school tomorrow.'

Vinay said, 'Why not? You will go to school.'

'In school, I will feel lonely. And I will think about my mother and you.'

Vinay said, 'No, you will not think about me and your mother. When you make friends there, then you will feel good at school.'

Payal said, 'When you will bring bicycle for me, I will go to school by bicycle.'

Vinay laughed and said, 'You will go to school by bicycle? I will definitely bring, but not for school, only for garden. You don't worry. Today I will bring you a bicycle. When you will grow up, don't forget us. Keep a bicycle always with you.

Payal said, 'I will stay with you. I will not marry.'

Vinay said, 'Payal, this is rule of society. We all have to marry and you too. Don't worry. When you feel bad there, call me.'

# 32

# Tears in Eyes and Bye-bye

Vinay's parents came to Mumbai. Vinay said, 'I had told you I will not stay without you. But you did not listen to me and sent me here alone. I was so lonely here.'

His mother took Vinay's head in her lap and said, 'Don't worry. We will stay with you.' She patted his head.

Vinay felt like he was in heaven. 'I have to live this moment with joy.' Vinay thought about his friends. 'I should have met my friends. This life is nothing without friends.' He was reminded of the faces of Jai and Archit. He thought about Tara and Lalita also. He thought, 'Lalita had loved me so much. But I did not care for her love.' Vinay was reminded of her pure love and the time that he had passed with her in his room. He remembered that she had come into his room without information. 'And she disturbed me jokingly and made excuses and came with me.' All these memories dwelled in her eyes.

When he had met Lalita the last time, she had said, 'Whenever you would need me, my heart would

196

be always open for you till the last breath.' His heart became heavy by this memory.

Then his mother said, 'Vinay, you are not well today.'

Vinay said, 'When I come to you, all my problems are solved automatically.' He said, 'How are you? How are my brother and sister-in-law?'

His mother said, 'They are calling you home. But you did not come.'

Vinay said, 'How are Jaya and Lalita?'

Vinay's mother said, 'They are good. Lalita has given birth to a boy and girl. Their names are Anish and Aaysha. Day before yesterday, they came to our home.'

He thought about his college life. 'I have enjoyed my life in college days.' Tears came into his eyes.

Vinay said to his mother, 'I am thinking about my college where I have studied. I am reminded of those days. I want to go again and study in college. But it is not possible. He said to himself, 'That time is never going to come back.' Vinay spoke to his mother about Lalita. 'I haven't told you. Once upon a time, I had to go to jail. Then Lalita got bail me. The same day, Lalita came to our home for the first time. I haven't paid duty of that obligation. If she will meet you again, then say to her that Vinay will definitely pay his duty.'

'Vinay, are you OK? What are you talking about?'

Vinay said, 'I am OK, Mom, I don't know what happened to me.'

Jaya said, 'From yesterday, Vinay is talking like this.'

Vinay's mother said, 'Don't worry. Everything will be OK.' Vinay called his driver and told him to bring a good bicycle for Payal.

Vinay saw his mother's eyes and prayed to God, 'Always keep my mother happy, please. Don't make her sad.'

Then somebody came to meet Vinay.

The guard informed Vinay, 'Someone wants to meet you.'

Vinay said, 'Send him inside. I will see him.'

Then the man came inside and said, 'Yesterday we had called you at Central Park. But you didn't come there.' He took out a pistol from his pocket and aimed at Vinay. But Jaya came in between, and he shot Jaya. Then he shot Vinay. And after that, he shot himself.

Seeing this, his parents lost consciousness. Payal swooned. Immediately, the guard came inside and called the police. The police came and took the pistol.

After seeing Vinay and Jaya, his mother started weeping; her eyes become tearful. She said, 'What happened? This was why you came to Mumbai? We were happy in the village.' She embraced Vinay.

His father was shocked on seeing this. Then Vinay said to his mother, 'For the last time, love me, my mother.' Hearing this, she kissed her son. 'Mother, I want to take my last breath at your feet.' His heart became very grief-stricken. Then Vinay died.

Police have taken their body for post-mortem. Then the police sent the body to the village. Vinay's brothers knew this, and they came to Vinay's village.

The news spread in the country that Vinay was no more.

Payal started weeping on seeing her uncle and aunt. She said, 'Uncle, don't go away from me.' She realised that her uncle would not come back. She said to herself, 'I will keep this bicycle always with me because this was given by you. And now who will take me to the city?' Her face became sad. Now she realised that he would never come back now.

The country went into mourning.

Many people came for Vinay's final journey and they sang the painful tune:

*Come and embrace me.*
*Sing this song together.*
*Don't trust on life.*
*Live it with full enjoy.*

The final traditional ritual was performed at the cremation ground of Vinay and Jaya.

That side, Payal and Vinay's mother felt grief at Vinay's death; they didn't feel good without Vinay. They didn't even like to eat food. Their health became poor.

Payal said to her grandma, 'My uncle will definitely come. He is in Mumbai right now.'

Vinay's mother said, 'He will never come. He made us weep and has gone forever.'

'Grandma, I think my uncle has gone to the city. Now he is coming. He never forgets my favourite. And see, his car is outside the house. He has a bag, and he is saying, "Payal, take your favourite." He will bring this time again.' Payal was saying this as she kept her head on her grandma's lap. And she started to drop pearls of tears from her eyes.

Seeing Payal like this, his mother felt the same grief for her son. She said, 'He will never come.'

Then Payal fell asleep in Grandma's lap.

Tara and Lalita too felt this grief of Vinay's and Jaya's death.

What happened after this?

1. Did Vinay get his love again or not?
2. Will Vinay take revenge on his enemy or not?
3. Will Lalita's love remain the same or will she become a widow?

# JAI SHRI MATAJI

## Sahaj yoga todays Mahayoga

Experience of self reliazation through kundalini awakening
Feel energy within us

Founder of Sahaj yoga Shri mataji Nirmala devi

Sahaj yoga is a unique methed of meditation based
on an experience called self realization (kundalini
awakening) that can occur within each human being.
Through this process an inner transformation takes place by
which one become moral united, integrated and balanced
One can actually feel the all pervading divine
power as a cool breeze, as described in all religions
and spiritual traditions of the world
This is the actualization of such transformation, which
is taking place now, worldwide, and has been proved and
experienced by thousands in over 90 country it is entirely free
of charge, as one cannot pay for the experience of divine love.
YOU CAN NOT KNOW THE MEANING OF
YOUR LIFE UNTIL YOU ARE CONNECTED
TO THE POWER THAT CREATED YOU
Experience now
Join sahaj yoga meditaion
www.sahajyoga.org.in
this is totaly free of cost

Please send your feedback to
shyamrathore1984@gmail.com